The Thursday Night Supper Club

Published by Seacoast Press, an imprint of MindStir Media, LLC

1931 Woodbury Ave. #182 | Portsmouth, New Hampshire 03801 | USA

1.800.767.0531 | www.seacoastpress.com

Printed in the United States of America

ISBN-13: 978-1-7376287-8-1

The Thursday Night Supper Club

AUDREY VALERIANI

SEACOAST
PRESS

Chapter 1

SILVIA CRUZ BOUNCED ALONG IN the back of a taxi that smelled like a combination of body odor and deli meats. The loud crackle of the driver's radio took her mind off the nausea, but her head pounded every time he hit a bump on Canal Street. As they zoomed around a corner, Silvia slid across the seat and slammed into the driver's side door. The sideways rain on this stormy March night in New York City didn't slow down the zig-zagging parade of travelers racing to reach their destinations. *Almost there.*

Finally, the taxi pulled over, and Silvia let out a deep sigh, grateful to have arrived at Liza's apartment. Here is where she would join her best friends for their girls' Thursday night dinner—her favorite night of the week. On these special occasions, these devoted women would meet here to enjoy a delicious, home-cooked meal, relax and connect with loved ones, and flip the bird to the world.

The driver pulled over and mumbled the price. It was always seventeen fifty, so Silvia jammed a twenty through the open slot and opened the door, anxious to get out into the fresh air. She grabbed her bag, held her coat over her head, and dodged raindrops as the cold propelled her quick steps to the front door. Once inside the hallway, she pushed the top floor bell and the buzzer went off almost immediately. *Now for the stairs.*

She took a deep breath to stave off the queasiness from the tortuous ride and bounded up the stairs as fast as she could. *Two, four, six, eight, ten*, she counted in her head. *Twelve, fourteen, sixteen, eighteen, landing,* and again, and again. At the top of the stairs, she was greeted by Liza who automatically handed her Little Bucket before entering the beloved sanctuary.

Liza's studio apartment was located in a quiet, unspoiled part of the city. The only downside was it was a fourth floor walk-up, but it was right across the street from the best pasta in the area and just a few blocks from the subway. At less than eight hundred square feet, Liza decorated it with love and a lavish, comfortable glamour only she could pull off—a sort of avant-garde hangout for sophisticated women. Among the most fascinating of her possessions was a giant, pink leopard, high heeled, shoe-shaped chair, which she carefully positioned in front of a window so it could be seen from the street. In the other corner, she hung a cream-colored, macramé chair that swung gently back and forth. Across from the windows all around a big comfy sofa and an overstuffed chair were many tiny, white scented candles flickering in the darkness to calm the soul of every visitor. Soft pillows scattered on the thick, white shag rug invited sore, weary feet to finally rest. The walls displayed some original artwork, and a slender stack of built-in shelves featured special collectibles, including oddly shaped framed pictures of loved ones, boxes of crazy sunglasses, and a selection of treasured souvenirs. Centered in the middle was Lulu—her beloved shiny, pink piggy bank she had kept with her since childhood and into which her friends stuffed money to help pay for the incredible feasts she prepared. Everyone loved being at this magical place that felt like the inside of a genie's bottle.

"Hi Sil!" Liza handed her Little Bucket and led her inside as she gagged on her way to the bathroom.

"Are you alright?"

"Yeah, I'll be out in a minute." Silvia splashed some cold water on her face, rinsed her mouth with a dab of toothpaste, then washed out Little Bucket and put it back under the sink. Unfortunately, she'd been prone to motion sickness since she was a kid. She dabbed a soft towel against her moist face and sighed. *Much better*. She turned and headed to the "sunroom"—a nickname they adopted to describe the <u>s</u>ecure, <u>u</u>nrestricted, and <u>n</u>onjudgmental space where they shared their innermost thoughts and feelings.

"No fair. You started without me." Silvia grabbed a cold bottle of water and slumped comfortably in her usual place among the pile of cushy pillows on the rug.

Tina leaned over and poked her. "Well, stop screwing around with the boss and leave work on time!"

"How else will I get promoted?" Silvia smiled and took a few sips of water. Her heart stopped racing, and her body began to feel normal again. "Okay, so fill me in. What's going on?"

"We were talking about a certain person's . . . boyfriend." Sarah tipped her head towards Julie who just happened to be sitting in a chair with a light shining directly in her face like a suspect in a 1940s police interrogation.

Silvia rolled her eyes. "Now what happened?"

"Well, this time he turned up at her place on Tuesday night at midnight while her sister was visiting. He was blind drunk and wanting—"

"A blowjob!"

"Ah!" Tina shrieked. "That's what I said!"

Liza, dressed in a long, shimmery green dress and gold slides, walked to the table carrying the largest platter of spaghetti and meatballs ever assembled prompting giant, toothy grins and grateful moans from her friends.

"No, nothing so naughty. He wanted money from her. Can you believe that?" She put her hands firmly on her hips. "The schmuck wanted her to give him money for a cab home after partying with his fakakta friends because he couldn't find his car! And turn off that light, it's ruining the ambient."

"You mean 'ambiance.'" Silvia turned back to the group. "Home where? He lives on the Island, doesn't he?"

"Yes, he does!" Sarah began filling her dish.

Julie punched a pillow. "Ugh! He was just so damned convinced he could sweet talk me . . . like I would fall to the floor with my legs in the air and my wallet wide open!"

Tina pointed her fork at her. "You know the guy is an asshole. I'm so glad your sister was there."

"Me too actually!" Julie giggled. "We were almost asleep. We had watched a movie and drank almost two bottles of wine. I was so happy to see my sister. We never get time together anymore . . . and then he shows up! He was plastered, although I have to admit we were a little buzzed too."

Silvia leaned in. "So what did Jen think?"

"She was pissed!" Julie sat up straight and adjusted her ponytail. "He was banging on the door, so I opened it and he practically fell in—tripped over the umbrella stand, fell down, and crawled along the floor and onto the couch. I told him to leave, but he said he needed money to get home, and then he asked for a glass of water.

When I came back with it, he was passed out with one pant leg stuck to a broken umbrella."

"He slept there? Julie!" Liza shook her head in disappointment.

"No! We kept calling his name and poking him, and he wouldn't move." She giggled again. "We realized then that he was out cold, so we decided to have a little fun. It was Jen's idea really, I swear."

Tina suddenly became more interested. "What do you mean?"

"Well, Jen grabbed her make-up case, and we put make-up on him!"

"What?" Liza screamed and fell back onto her chair.

"We gave him dramatic eyebrows—kind of like what's her name . . . Mommy Dearest."

"No wire hangers!" shouted Tina.

"We even glued on false eyelashes!" The girls were all laughing. "We styled his hair too. Well, by styled I mean . . . my sister gave him bangs!"

"Fucking brilliant!" Tina high-fived her friend.

"And look!" Julie fumbled with her phone. "We took a picture!"

The image of the smug, muscle-bound moron made everyone laugh until they cried. Silvia finally managed to take a deep breath. "And he didn't wake up?"

"No! When we were done, I didn't want him waking up in my apartment, so I grabbed his phone and found a number labeled 'Home' and called it."

"Who answered?" Liza was rocking back and forth and almost fell off the giant shoe.

"His mother answered—"

"She called his mother!" Sarah clapped with delight.

"When she answered, I apologized for the late hour. I told her that her son was sick and couldn't get home on his own and asked if she could come pick him up. About half an hour later, she arrived.

9

She gasped when she saw him. We acted like there wasn't anything different about him," Julie squealed, "and helped her get him down the stairs and into her car! The poor woman was mortified. She could smell the booze on him."

"A-a-a-h, I love it!" Tina was impressed by sweet Julie's deeply hidden evil genius.

"We're so proud of you!" Silvia raised her hands over her head as though Julie just scored a goal.

"I'd still like to cut his balls off!" Liza mumbled while stabbing a meatball and adding it to her plate.

"I'm never going to find a decent guy! No one's ever going to love me again." Julie curled up on the pillows next to Silvia.

"Don't say things like that. Quick, spit away the back luck. Pooh, pooh, pooh! You don't want to attract the evil eye! Do it!" Julie reluctantly sat up and dry spit into the air.

Tina shook her head. "Again with this crazy fucking superstition?"

Liza glared at Tina. "All cultures have traditions. Chinese people have their fortune cookies, and we spit away the bad luck. It works! Jews have been spitting for centuries—as long as your fortune cookies have been around!"

Tina jumped to her feet in frustration. "Oh my God! Fortune cookies did not come from China! Read some history once in a while instead of just *Vogue* and *The Fran Drescher Story*!"

"How dare you!" Liza tried to be serious, but burst out laughing, breaking the tension. Everyone then began imitating Fran's character on the television show, *The Nanny*.

While Tina and Liza pretended to battle it out, Julie and Silvia helped themselves to another portion of the wonderful Italian feast and poured more wine from the lovely crystal decanter set in the middle of the table. Though Liza didn't always present the best execution of the English language, her esthetic presentations made her dinners a visual as well as culinary delight.

"What are you eating now?" Silvia tried to open Liza's closed hand.

"What? Just some red hot candies."

Silvia shook her head. "I swear, you are addicted to those things!"

"I can quit any time I want."

Tina laughed. "Sure. Red Hots? I'm surprised she doesn't scream every time she poops!"

"Okay, girls. Come on and listen." Liza wiped her hands and held up her glass prompting the others to do the same. "Cheers! To my wonderful girls who love and support me no matter what crazy things I do!"

Oh-oh. Silvia's heart skipped a beat as they raised their glasses.

Tina dropped her head. "Oh God. What did you do this time?"

"Tell us!" Julie was excited to hear all about Liza's latest exploits.

"Well, girls. You all know I believe in moving forward in life, right? Trying new things . . . always reinventing myself."

Changing jobs a lot. Silvia raised her eyebrows at Liza. "Yes, go on."

"Well . . ." Liza stood up and took a deep breath. "I'm going to be a stand-up comedian!"

For a moment, no one spoke. However, the whites of four sets of wide eyes glowing in the candlelight spoke volumes.

"Are you serious? A stand-up—" Sarah was shocked.

"Really? That's very interesting!" Julie smiled and nodded politely.

Tina remained unmoved. "Whatever blows your dress up. Can someone please pass the salt?"

"Yes! You girls know I'm funny. I'm the 'artiste extraordinary' of our group. So I thought, now that I'm retired from Con-Ed" (*Laid off,* Silvia thought) "and only working part-time at the boutique"

(*Discount store*), "I decided to put some material together and try stand-up comedy."

Silvia was surprised. "That's 'artiste extraordinaire' and . . . What?"

"I mean, don't get me wrong, I know I have a lot to learn. I have to write some funny jokes and test my material on lots of people before I could actually make a living at this. And I know it's a long shot, but with some practice, I know . . . I just know this is my calling. I truly believe I am destined to become a comedy star!" She reached up with both hands for dramatic effect.

Liza appeared serious, although the girls were used to her sudden epiphanies as well as their eventual lackluster demise. However, it was always fun to go along for the ride. Who knows where this would lead?

"Really?" Sarah seemed concerned. "Actually make a living—?"

"I think it's fabulous. What gave you the idea?" Silvia smiled and leaned in closer to Liza. She had never seen her so excited.

"Well, I was watching a show on Lifetime about women and their second chances—you know, women who were starting a new career later in life . . . like after their husbands divorced them or their grown children left the nest. So I wondered if that was something I might try. Then I thought about what I really love—making people laugh and making fun of things, ego—"

"Ergo," whispered Silvia.

"Stand-up comedian!"

"I think you'll be a smash for sure!" Tina smiled and tried to sound convincing but needed a lot more wine to keep her logical mind from exploding.

"Oh girls, you really think so?" Liza bounced up and down in her seat.

Following Silvia's example (and the threatening look on her face), the girls quickly jumped into support mode with lots of encouragement. They praised Liza's quick wit and mused about her eventual fame and fortune. They even play-acted interviewing her on a talk show by using a rolled-up newspaper as a microphone.

"So Ms. Levy, please tell our audience how long you dreamed of becoming a comedian."

"Oh, I'd have to say since I was . . . about thirty-two."

"And how long did it take you to become famous?"

"Oh, gosh, a while . . . almost three months!"

"And being in such high demand, how do you spend your precious down time?"

"Well, I drive around with Jerry Seinfeld and hang out with Chris Rock and Amy Schumer too. Oh, and Sarah Silverman's house—a triumph! You see, I've completely forgotten where I came from and who my friends are!" Liza had everyone in stitches, and this precious, playful interaction and reassurance was exactly what she needed.

On the way home, Silvia kept thinking about her friend's newest obsession. The idea seemed to come out of nowhere, but after more consideration, it was a natural, albeit unconventional, choice for her. Liza was the funniest person she knew. Everyone loved her and her irrepressible quick wit. She was usually the center of attention at parties and had proven over and over she could deliver a punchline, so why not? She could be the break-out star of the bunch.

Chapter 2

SILVIA CRUZ WAS A CHARMING, attractive brunette with an enviable figure. She had long, wavy hair which she often wore up, high cheekbones, and long eyelashes. She maintained an outward appearance of confidence with her smiling eyes and easy laugh and had a formidable sense of integrity. Those around her reveled in her warmth, compassion, and helpful nature. What no one knew, however, was that inside she was insecure and distrustful of most people, and it took a lot of work to keep those feelings tightly under wraps.

From the age of eighteen, Silvia worked to support herself. Some of her first jobs were waitress, retail salesclerk, and receptionist. Finally, she realized she wanted a "career in words" as she described it. She wanted to be a writer. Knowing an advanced education was vital in realizing her dream, she financed two years of community college through grants, student loans, and by working two jobs: a secretarial assistant during the day and a bartender at night. During her third year, her exemplary grades won her a job placement at the *Brooklyn Daily Eagle*. At that time, she was just asked to do errands and help around the office, but she went to work every day smiling and enthusiastic. She had gotten her foot in the door at a place where the air was electric, creativity was flowing, and people were actually getting paid to write!

After more diligent study and student-poor years, she finally received a BA from CUNY, which prompted her to hunt for a job more in step with her dream of becoming a writer. Eventually she landed a job at the *New York Post* where she ascended from office assistant to her current job as a proofreader. As she delved into her assignments, she hoped one day she would create her own masterpiece—something that would make people think or perhaps even change people's lives. She also loved creating characters who embarked on all sorts of wild adventures, and though she longed to share her passion, nothing she wrote had been seen by anyone. Even the articles she wrote and submitted for publication were kept private, choosing to wait for validation and accolades from the publishing community before opening herself up to the criticism of loved ones.

Silvia had one big love in her life, but after a few years she realized she was just repeating past patterns. He turned out to be a non-spiritual, immature man-child whose only goal was to have the most fun before he died without regard for consequences. He was irresponsible with money and turned cold when a situation called for love and compassion. It took several years for her to realize that her quest for a happy ending caused her to imagine integrity in someone when it was just not there.

Now at twenty-nine years old, her job, good movies, and spending time with her girlfriends completed Silvia's simple, drama-free world. It had taken an enormous effort over many years to get to this place, but she managed to create a functioning world where she felt somewhat safe and capable of maneuvering through the challenges life presented. She was a sensitive and logical person who felt most comfortable sticking to a routine and in familiar surroundings. Her close group of girlfriends meant the world to her, and in them she found the keys to expanding her life skills and maintaining her sanity.

Silvia was the informal founder of their little supper club. Soon after she met each of these women, it became clear to her that they possessed varied perspectives on life, the best of intentions, and individual talents that, when combined and shared, could benefit them all. An intimate sisterhood seemed to form naturally—one they all cherished and depended on more and more as time went on.

Silvia met Liza Levy at the Angel Street Thrift Shop, a non-profit secondhand store where the rich sought to absolve themselves for foolishly wasting their millions. They began chatting and immediately liked one another. Before leaving, Liza purchased a long, crystal beaded cape—one Silvia thought only Liberace could pull off—which sparked a curiosity in her to get to know this oddly enchanting woman. Liza's capability to see humor in everything and her uninhibited spontaneity amazed her. More importantly, her lack of concern about the opinions of others was inconceivable to Silvia, and she had to learn more.

Liza was a very Jewish and devoted daughter of her beloved city. From the moment you heard her thick accent and saw her funky clothing, you could almost hear Frank Sinatra singing "New York, New York." She was the oldest in their group of friends, and her role could be described as either glamorous guru or bubbe. She stood five feet four inches and weighed two hundred pounds but appeared to be the antithesis of middle-aged stereotypes by maintaining her youthful wonder and curiosity about life. She wore minimal make-up on her round face but could always be found wearing her signature red lipstick. She loved large jewelry, hats, and vintage clothing—really anything shocking or dramatic.

Liza bounced from job to job over the years, never aspiring to become a lawyer or an accountant or even a hairdresser. She believed in following life as it unfolded. She perceived every day as an adventure and expected great things to come her way. She had a knack for surprising those who underestimated her, turning heads with her fashion choices, and making the best of everything.

After her favorite aunt, Gerdy, died, Liza inherited her apartment and had been living there for about eight years. Gerdy was the aunt who begged Liza's mother to name her daughter "Liza" for Liza Minnelli. At the time of her birth, the movie *Cabaret* had just opened in theaters, and both sisters loved the movie and the actress. Her mother, however, wasn't so eager to name her daughter after such a decadent character. "You want I should name my daughter after a nafka?" asked her mother. "No," said Gerdy, "she'll be named after the actress, not the whore!"

Liza was very charismatic and had easily acquired many friends and acquaintances over the years, though none knew her pain. She had been criticized most of her life for her weight and her refusal to conform to society's norms. Liza knew she was born to be different and no amount of sweet-talking or ridicule from her family would ever change that. All it did was push her further away.

Liza's only other close friend was Thomas, a gorgeous gay man with whom she had previously worked and on whom she secretly had a crush. He was tall, had wavy brown hair, chiseled features, and a dimple in his chin like Tom Selleck. He knew of Liza's struggles and inner loneliness and considered her a cherished friend. However, because of conflicting schedules and differing lifestyles, they rarely got to spend much time together. They maintained their relationship with late night kvetching on their cell phones and the occasional weekend outing. Though she had Thomas and a few crazy old aunts who checked in from time to time, Liza considered these four women friends her real family with whom she felt accepted and loved, and able to freely live her life in any form and as she saw fit.

Silvia met Julie Ward after literally bumping into her outside of Macy's. Julie had been shopping to ease the pain of a break-up and slammed into Silvia on the way out of the store. Silvia was worried about the frantic woman's state of mind and took her for a cup of coffee to talk. She listened to her stories of lost love and was bowled over by her pure, open heart and its amazing resiliency. However, it was the beauty of Julie's overall vulnerability that was like a lightning bolt hitting Silva square in the chest.

Julie was a small, cute blonde with blue eyes who worked as a compliance analyst at the IRS. She wore a variety of relaxed suits to work almost every day but took her job seriously. She had a nice apartment, a fairly busy social life, and earned a living wage that allowed her a healthy supply of her favorite wine and the means to have a little fun once in a while. She came from a loving, slightly pretentious family who had strong morals and values. Her mother was a librarian at a Catholic school, and her father was an engineer who also taught catechism school on Sundays.

Julie was quirky and naïve and mostly happy in her life, although romantic relationships were challenging for her and her family knew it. Her parents had urged her to find a "nice boy" and settle down, but her choices in men were far from their ideal. They introduced her to successful, acceptable candidates, but each time she rejected one she felt their disappointment in her. She felt smothered and as though she could never live up to their expectations. Though she admittedly had a wonderful family, she never felt like she fit in with their black and white set of rules to live by or their *Leave It to Beaver* existence. In her close women friends, Julie found like-minded, caring individuals who cultivated her bohemian approach to love and life.

Julie introduced Silvia to her new friend, Sarah Green, one day at lunch. Sarah's guarded, professional demeanor did little to hide her vulnerable interior to a keen observer, and that protection of self and fear of being rejected endeared her to Silvia.

Sarah stood five feet eight inches and was slim with shoulder length brown hair. She had pale white skin, large brown eyes, and a lovely smile. She appeared to be a woman comfortable with the status quo, however just beneath the surface simmered a curiosity for something more. She was a kind, straightforward person who worked hard at her job as assistant manager at the New York City Records Department. Though she hated her boss and didn't make a lot of money, she loved that her job title elevated her above the level of "staff" and required her to supervise about a dozen subordinates. Follow the rules and never fart in public—that was Sarah.

While she had a few relatives in New York, most of Sarah's family lived in Philadelphia, where she was born and continued to visit every so often. She had distanced herself from her home and relatives on purpose a few years ago. Alcoholism and drug abuse were prevalent in her family, and their bad choices and negative attitudes became toxic for her. She felt depressed and stifled and as though there was someone else trying to emerge from inside herself. She craved peace and positivity and decided to find a better way to live. Sarah finally made the move to New York and eventually met these exceptional women. She came to realize that her girlfriends were the only people who were stable and dependable in her life. She found they sensed, understood, and lovingly nurtured her need for support and her simmering transformation.

Finally, after being together for a while, the four women met Tina Chin when they got together for a little pampering at a salon called Santé. She came into their lives like a hurricane. She was a woman keenly focused on her success through hard work, education, and never taking her eye off the prize. She exuded confidence and made a huge impression on them after eloquently declaring her dream to the group (and giving them all a large quantity of beauty samples). Silvia was extremely impressed by this well put together woman. She seemed to have been shaken back to life by Tina's passion and energy and became invigorated and refocused on her own dream of becoming a writer.

Tina was a small, pretty, fashion-conscience dynamo who was in charge of two departments at Santé: Make-up Design and Hair Creations. She was always perfectly made-up, had a great personal style, and was a natural born leader. She was the daughter of Chinese American parents who tried to keep her tied to their old-world customs. Although she respected her family's traditions, she grew up feeling and thinking differently than her relatives and became ultra-focused on achieving her independence. She was intelligent, fiercely loyal, and had an outrageous sense of humor. She was direct and never sugarcoated the truth but also possessed a sensitivity for the underdog, which was often obscured by her strong, confident facade. Engaging with this diverse group of women was like a breath of fresh air for Tina. Unlike her family, her new friends respected and encouraged her ambitious spirit and even understood that those who didn't appear to need anyone or anything were often the people who needed love and support most of all.

These four wonderful women with different backgrounds, experiences, and ambitions inspired Silvia to improve herself and slowly grew into the loving family she never had.

Chapter 3

THE NEXT FEW WEEKS WERE busy for everyone, but the girls finally managed to meet up at Liza's on Thursday for dinner. Silvia arrived last and was welcomed by Liza who was dressed in a brightly colored, knee-length dress, a statement necklace, and lots of big bracelets. After utilizing Little Bucket, Silvia joined her friends in the sunroom for another exquisite meal. The menu this week was a Tex-Mex feast paired with mouthwatering margaritas.

"What a week I had!" Silvia closed her tired eyes as she kicked off her shoes and sipped her perfectly mixed cocktail. "Oh, so good!"

"I hear that!" Tina raised her glass to her. "I'm so sick of listening to those lifted faces complain about everything. They even bitch about the color of the friggin' towels in the sauna! It takes all my willpower not to whack them in their perfectly straightened noses!"

"Oh my God! That must be so hard for you!" Sarah teased.

"It is!" Tina giggled. "Honestly, most of the other ladies are nice. There's just this one woman who is such a—"

"I know what you're thinking, and don't say it," warned Liza.

"Fine. Her name is Irene friggin' Piper. We call her the 'Viper' because she's so mean. She comes in every week for tanning, extensions, and gel nails—everything really. She's one of those women who married rich, is desperate to regain her youth, and annoys everyone with her obvious attempts at manipulation with fake compliments. She uses lots of 'darlings' and 'sweethearts.' She drives me fucking crazy!" Tina then changed her demeanor.

"But then there's Mrs. Klein. She's this sweet, old lady who is always pleasant and smiles at everyone. And this clique of bloated, vodka-soaked New York trophy wives—whose leader is none other than Viper—make fun of this genuinely kind, lovely woman because she doesn't come in wearing Gucci or smelling like Chanel No. 5."

"Wow. The place sounds so friendly." Sarah rolled her eyes.

"For example—"

Liza sat forward. "Oh, good. There's more."

"Today the Viper comes in and tells Mrs. Klein that she usually sits where Mrs. Klein was sitting. She makes her get up . . . chases her off . . . actually clapping her hands and saying, 'quick as a bunny!'" She makes air quotes. "So poor Mrs. Klein jumps up, apologizes, and walks toward the foyer not knowing where else to go. I mean, the balls on that woman!" Tina's anger showed on her flushed face.

"So nasty!" Julie closed her eyes and shook her head.

"May her fake lips dry up into raisins!" Liza chanted, as if casting a spell.

"Yeah, that's not right." Silvia leaned forward resting her elbows on her knees. "She's a bully. You can't let her get away with that shit."

"You know, some green dye could accidentally find its way into her facial! Then she would have to go back to her home planet!" Liza giggled and clapped her hands with delight at her scheme.

"Yes, that's exactly what I want." Tina smiled at the thought. "Why won't she just go gently into that good Florida?"

"Oh, Florida!" Sarah jumped off the giant shoe. "Thanks for reminding me. I forgot to tell you guys. I have to go to Florida."

"Have to?" The news captivated Liza. "Where? Miami? Why?"

"No, not Miami. I have to go to this stupid two-day, executive, administrator, manager training bullshit thingy next month. And it's mandatory that I go, as I was told by my supervisor—"

"Mary Louise!" All the girls screamed her name with revulsion.

Sarah rubbed her hands together like a villain. "Yup. Mary Louise . . . the Lex Luthor to my Superman; the Green Goblin to my Spider-Man; the Joker to my Batman—!"

"We get it, Doctor Who Cares!" Tina waved at her to stop.

"O-o-h!" Liza shouted. "Word play on superheroes! What about . . . the Wizard of Oddballs? Fire Fart! And Dead Fool!"

"Or . . . the Toxic Vagina!" Silvia shouted and rolled onto the pillows, laughing at her own stupid joke.

"Thanks a lot, you guys!" Sarah got up to get another margarita, and the girls eventually stopped laughing and offered their apologies.

"Anyway, she told me I desperately needed some leadership training and had to learn how to communicate with people, and those were the words she used to my face. I heard from one of the staff what she actually said behind my back was that my supervisory skills were atrocious. She also said she wondered why Mr. Casey even promoted me . . . but she had her suspicions given the time we spend together in his office! Can you believe that?"

Julie gasped. "That is just—"

"To what was she inferring?" Liza stood up and put her hands on her hips.

"Implying," corrected Silvia. Liza looked confused.

"I know! She's basically saying that I screwed Casey for my job! The truth is he calls me into his office to discuss reports and assignments because he can't fucking stand her!"

"Now that's not funny!" Tina was riled. "She's screwing with your professional reputation!"

Julie nodded in disgust. "She must have a heck of a reputation herself! She's so mean, and didn't you say she wore big ugly shoes?"

"Yeah! They're a combination of ortho-chic and combat boots!"

"I think we should take the bitch out?" Liza spoke like a tough-talking New Yorker.

"Anyway, now I have to attend this training, and well, there's supposed to be a reception and a pool party, and oh, I don't know . . ." Sarah's face turned red, and she began to shake.

"But it's in Florida. Florida!" Liza couldn't believe anyone would object to a trip there for any reason.

Julie pointed her finger at Sarah. "You know, in my opinion, I think she's doing you a favor. At least you'll get away for a few days."

"It'll be okay, Sarah. Calm down. Let's see . . ." Silvia looked up at the ceiling waiting for God to beam down an idea. "Hey! We can go shopping this weekend and get you some fabulous, new, confidence-building outfits. You'll be a knock-out!" Silvia smiled and punched her fists in the air like a boxer.

"Oh fun! I wish I could go, but I have no extra money to spend at the moment . . . car repairs, ya know." Julie frowned.

"You should just sell it. You hardly ever use it." Tina shrugged.

"I really can't right now, either. You know how busy I am working on my comedy." Liza never went shopping with the girls. They always shopped in stores that very seldom carried her size or her style. Besides, she always found her magnificently unique outfits at secret locations around the city, which she preferred to keep to herself.

Tina nodded. "And I'll have to work too, I'm sure."

"That's okay." Silvia smiled. "We'll go ourselves. You'll probably need a new swimsuit and a cocktail dress to wear to the events. How's that sound?"

"Thank you, Sil. I'm just sick over this." Sarah covered her face with her hands.

Tina smiled. "And I'll grab you some new designer make-up samples to try out."

Liza stopped and leaned over to Tina. She was almost salivating at the mere mention of free designer cosmetics. "Can I have some too?"

Tina winked and nodded at Liza, then continued offering help to Sarah. "And if you can, stop by the spa this week and we can practice applying your make-up before you go. Just call ahead, alright?"

"And who knows? There's bound to be some men there. Maybe you'll even meet someone!" Julie clapped excitedly.

"Oh God!" Sarah jumped up and ran into the bathroom.

"Nice work."

Liza moved into the center of the group. "Okay girls, I have to tell you all something. Sarah, please come back here."

Silvia jumped up. "Wait, I need another margarita!"

Liza put her head down and folded her hands until the group came back together. "Unfortunately, as you all know, sometimes bad things happen to good people."

Silvia rolled her eyes. *Always with the quoting.*

"While I wish I had news about my bludgeoning" (*Burgeoning*, thought Silvia) "career, what I have to tell you is . . ." Liza closed her eyes and took a deep breath. "My aunt called me before canceling her mahjong game this morning and told me . . . my Uncle Morty died. Uncle Morty is dead, girls!"

Silvia took Liza's hand. "I'm so sorry."

"Oh, that's too bad. He was so funny." Julie sat up from relaxing on the couch.

"No, not Uncle Morty." Tina pouted. "I loved that guy!"

"I know, we all did. He passed in his sleep . . . they think from an aneurism in the head. Very sad. My Aunt Eunice is so distraught. She says she can't be in the apartment without him. She's already made plans to go stay with her sister-in-law in Miami right after the church service." Liza reached for a tissue and dabbed her eyes.

"Church service?" Julie was confused. "But he was Jewish, right? Don't they do shiva or something?"

"Yeah, shiva," explained Liza, "but we have a mixed family and my Aunt Eunice said she was too inconsolable to argue about tradition. The rest of them are all fighting like a bunch of mental patients! All I know is my Uncle Morty is going to be buried tomorrow morning, and then there'll be a memorial service at St. Bartholomew's Church at three o'clock. Can I count on all you girls attending?"

"Attending?" Tina winced. She was very uncomfortable with anything having to do with death and dying . . . and freakishly long toes and back acne.

"Yes, I gotta have my girls there! I know how you all loved Uncle Morty," Liza continued with raised eyebrows, "especially because he was so generous to all of us." She paused for a moment so the girls could respond.

Julie grinned, Sarah sighed, and Tina scratched her head.

"Of course, we'll be there." Silvia patted Liza's knee.

"Remember when he gave us all those fur coats he got from the trunk of . . . I mean, his friend's going out of business sale a few years ago? And how he got us those tickets to see Barry. Uncle Morty . . . always so thoughtful, right?"

Silvia looked at Tina with the stern face of an old parochial school nun. "It was third row center for Barry Manilow!"

"I don't know if I can go. I have to work." Sarah dreaded asking Mary Louise for time off.

"Where is it again?" Silvia took out her calendar and whispered to Sarah, "Screw Mary Louise!"

Sarah scowled. "No, thank you. I'll just take emergency personal time instead."

"St. Bartholomew's Church at three tomorrow," repeated Liza. The girls reluctantly acquiesced and began to reminisce about the good times they had with Uncle Morty.

Liza chuckled and grabbed a handful of red hot candies. "Hey, remember when Uncle Morty showed up at my Aunt Mimi's house at the shore that time she let us use it for the weekend? He said he came to check on the house, but I think he just wanted to come out and play with us girls without his nagging wife!"

"Oh yeah!" Silvia chuckled. "He showed up looking like an extra from *Baywatch*! We're sitting there and look up to see this half-bald guy—his comb-over blowing in the wind—running on the beach toward us wearing a muscle t-shirt, bright colored shorts, and carrying a bottle of Johnny Walker wrapped in a giant beach towel!" Then giving her best impersonation of Uncle Morty, she added with a gruff voice, "I gotta check the pipes aren't leaking, check the roof's not caving in . . ." The girls all screamed with laughter.

"And make sure there weren't any schmucks around, I'm sure! God forbid!" Liza shook her head.

Julie relaxed back on the couch. "And he stayed all day drinking with us on the beach."

Sarah looked confused unable to remember the occasion.

"Sarah, I think you were home with toe fungus or an ingrown toenail. It had something to do with your feet, I remember that!" Tina shuddered.

"We got so drunk, and he got hammered too and couldn't drive home. So we fed him some dinner hoping he would sober up. The next thing we know, he's passed out on the big couch on the porch!" Liza snorted thinking about the lovable old fool.

Silvia turned to Sarah. "It was hilarious! He was out there snoring like a big bear! I felt bad for the neighbors!"

"So we threw a cotton blanket on him and left him there while we partied on!" Liza giggled. "And in the morning when we got up, he was gone! I thought my aunt was gonna kill him, honest to God!" Everyone laughed.

"Oh!" Silvia gasped. "Liza, remember the time Uncle Morty tried to fix me up with that guy?"

"Oh, that's right! Benny the Bet! Oh my God, girls, you should have seen the guy he wanted to set her up with. I knew who he was, so I stopped it."

"Thank God!"

"Benny the Bet was another giant in the dry cleaning business and a big time gambler." Liza giggled. "He was only about five feet five and wore these awful polyester suits with ugly, worn out, brown tassel shoes! And he smoked cigars constantly . . . chewed on them too." The girls laughed and shrieked with disgust.

"And what's really funny is . . . he said he wore polyester suits because . . ." Liza laughed hysterically while trying to finish her thought, ". . . they didn't have to be dry cleaned!" The girls roared.

The group continued listening to Liza tell amusing stories about her beloved uncle. By the time she was done straightening his halo and bleaching his angel wings, all the girls agreed they must attend Uncle Morty's memorial service. Persistent Jewish persuasion triumphs once again!

The next afternoon, the girls gathered at St. Bartholomew's Church for Uncle Morty's memorial service. The place was packed with solemn-looking Catholics and annoyed-looking Jews. Liza's cousin, David, kept staring at the giant crucifix hanging from the ceiling like he was waiting for it to drop on his head and kill him for slandering Jesus Christ. After spending some time talking with her family at the front of the church, Liza, dressed in a long black dress with a rhinestone collar and pillbox hat, joined her friends already sitting together in a pew several rows back.

"Thank you for coming, girls." Liza wiped tears from her eyes. "Poor Uncle Morty." Her friends reached out to comfort her.

"How's your Aunt Eunice?" Silvia patted Liza's hand.

"She's upset, of course, as we all are. And she's very uneasy about mixing her Catholic cousins with Morty's Jews here in this church. And she keeps saying she needs time away . . . got her luggage in the trunk of the Caddy. She's leaving for Miami tonight. Just now she tells us that her sister-in-law, the big time realtor, has a condo for her to look at down there. I don't think she knows what she's doing right now." Liza shook her head. "The woman loses a husband and tries to escape the pain and grief with palm trees and cabana boys."

"And serial killers." Tina shrugged off the glaring looks from her friends.

"I'll tell you, my old Aunt Ida is not pleased with her having a Catholic memorial service and leaving so soon for Florida. Ida is just beside herself having to be here—she keeps clutching at her heart. And I think she cursed Eunice in Yiddish!"

Silvia pointed toward the front of the church. "Who's that woman with the big hat on?"

"That's Aunt Catherine." Liza grimaced. "I guess she's a bigwig in this church. I just heard she organizes the church's beauty pageants and bike trails. She's acting like she's the boss of everyone, which is really pissing off all the Jews."

"I think you might mean she organizes the Christmas pageants and bake sales." Sarah held up the piece of paper she was holding. "It's all explained here in the church bulletin." Liza grabbed the circular from Sarah and started fanning herself with it while the girls began to fidget. It was already becoming very warm in the church.

"Whatever! You know what else she did? She went over to greet some of my Jewish aunts and uncles when they arrived and suggested they not eat the, the . . . cookie or drink any wine that might be offered to them by a priest, or they would go to hell! Can you believe that? Talked to them like they were goddamned Mormons!"

Julie looked confused. "Jewish people know about the wafers and wine . . . the body and blood of Christ, right?'"

"Yes, all that nonsense." Liza was agitated by her aunt's callousness and the increasing heat in the church. "And we don't even believe in hell! It just would have been nice if she made them feel welcome, that's all. And her hat is fucking ridiculous!"

Sarah's head spun around. "So there's going to be a full Mass?"

"Well, Catherine wasn't sure what the priest and my Aunt Eunice had planned exactly because they're not speaking. That woman— such chutzpah!"

"I thought chutzpah was a good thing?" asked Tina.

"No, not really."

Once the service began, it became clear there would be no Mass—just a long, grueling recounting of the highs and lows of Uncle Morty's eccentric life by his loved ones. In fact, a Mass would have been shorter. By the time the third speaker concluded his mind-numbing homage to Uncle Morty, the girls were hot, bored, and restless. However, not even the extreme humidity in the church could stop the tributes from continuing.

More and more friends and family got up and told their own personal stories about Morty, the man. Some were altruistic: "That man always took time out of his busy day to come visit my wife when I was out of town"; some, sentimental: "That little pisher kicked me in the nuts when I was a kid, but I loved him like a brother"; and some, facetious: "I feel bad we all lost Morty, but I'm happy Eunice is finally getting what she always wanted . . ." Then, after some criticism from the crowd, the speaker clarified his remark. "What? She's getting a condo in Florida!"

While what seemed like the hundredth speaker recalled what Uncle Morty was like in the early days of the laundry and dry cleaning business, Sarah sighed loudly. "Oh my God! There's no air in here. When is this going to end?"

"I know, I'm sweating my cha-cha off." Liza opened her legs wide, then took out her monogrammed handkerchief and wiped the sweat off her neck.

"Look at this poor guy!" Tina gestured to an old man sitting in front of them who had sweat rolling down from under his hideous hairpiece. He also wore thick dark glasses and a beard. As they looked at the comical, archetypical sight, the girls started to get the giggles.

In an obvious effort to entertain her bored friends, Julie pointed her finger right behind the man's head several times, each time getting closer and closer to the unruly mess. All of a sudden, Tina leaned over and shoved Julie's elbow forward, slamming her hand into the back of the man's head and moving his hairpiece off to the side.

At the precise moment the speaker at the podium called Uncle Morty "a Legend in Laundry," the eruption of laughter from the girls' pew caused the church full of Catholics and Jews alike to stop and turn toward them. Although the girls were embarrassed that their blasphemous conduct was exposed, they continued to exhibit the kind of behavior that could only be described as psychotic hysteria. No amount of scolding from the elders sitting in front of them could quiet the girls. In fact, their reprimands only augmented the disturbing sounds erupting from the five sinful women sitting in the now damned pew. Unable to quiet themselves, the girls covered their mouths while scuffling sideways out of the pew, and then sprinted down the side aisle of St. Bartholomew's Church.

Outside the church, they unleashed full-blown fits of laughter at their wildly inappropriate participation in the desecration of a laundry legend. Falling onto one other on the church steps, hot and spent, Silvia struggled to get the group back up and under control, but it was no use. And once Liza announced to the group that she peed her pants, it was all over. "I gotta go home now, girls," she roared. "Jesus, help me. I gotta go home!"

Chapter 4

UNFORTUNATELY, THE GIRLS WEREN'T ABLE to meet for dinner the following Thursday night, so on Saturday they met for an early breakfast before Silvia and Sarah went on their shopping spree. They were all eager to hear about the fall-out from the debacle at the memorial.

"So has your family disowned you?" Tina grinned at Liza.

"I can't believe you did that to Julie!" Sarah pushed Tina's shoulder. "Of all people . . . the little Catholic girl whose father is a Sunday school teacher!"

"I know! I'd like to say my arm has a mind of its own but . . ." Tina giggled while eating her omelet.

"I've never laughed so hard!" Silvia touched her forehead. "I feel like I should go to confession for that!"

"And I peed myself!" Liza wiped tears streaming down her face. "My underwear . . . my dress! Oh, that was hilarious. I wonder what Uncle Morty thought of what we did."

"I'm sure he was laughing his ass off!" Silvia smiled and blew a kiss up to the lovable rascal in heaven.

"My family was so pissed! The shit I had to take from my relatives. You have no idea the names they called me—and you! My

Aunt Eunice has forbidden me to attend the reading of Morty's will next month!" Liza chuckled. "She never wants to see me again, so that's one good thing that came of it anyway!" A burst of laughter filled the booth. "And I know it was long and boring, but I'm glad you were all there with me. It meant a lot."

Julie sipped her coffee. "Hey, who was the hairpiece guy, anyway?"

"An old friend of my uncle. I think he used to be a bookie and maybe a loan shark back in the day. I feel bad . . . the poor old guy!"

"Are you shitting me?" Sarah dropped her fork.

"That explains the cheap disguise!" Tina slapped the table.

After a few minutes, the girls returned to eating and sharing the giant stack of waffles ordered by tiny Julie.

"So what else is new?" Julie looked at Sarah who didn't appear to be enjoying herself as much as the others. "Are you okay?"

"Old Combat Boots is driving me nuts!" Sarah put her head in her hands. "I'm about ready to walk out, I swear! The other day, I was covering the main desk for the whole day, handling everything perfectly fine while she was at an executive meeting. I even skipped lunch. Finally, at three-thirty I was starving, so I ran to the cafeteria to grab a sandwich. Of course, that's when Mary Louise returned to the desk."

"Figures, right?" Tina shook her head.

"As I got off the elevators, she sees me . . . walks halfway across the floor toward me with her arms crossed and says, 'Where have you been?' She's just such an asshole."

Julie sat straight up. "What did you say back?"

"I told her where I was, and that I hadn't moved from the desk all day, except for these lousy few minutes to run and grab some food— but it didn't matter. She stormed away towards Casey's office."

Silvia waved her hand. "Oh, he knows how she is!"

"I hate her like poison!" Liza shook her head while cutting into her sausage.

"Wow, Liza. I thought you would have said what you always say: 'Let it go, and don't carry a grudge because . . . it weighs a lot and doesn't have a handle!'" The girls finished the quote together, as Silvia led them like the conductor of a symphony.

"Fuck that shit. This is war!"

Tina pushed her empty plate away and leaned back. "I agree with Liza! Sarah, you gotta get out of there . . . or at least get her back somehow!"

"How? What can I do?" Sarah shrugged. She had never intentionally hurt anyone in her life.

Tina sighed and glared at her. "We can slice her tires!"

Julie pounded her fist. "We can egg her house!"

Sarah mumbled, "We can post her phone number on an S&M website."

"Okay, enough of this nonsense. I'm officially changing the subject." Liza poured herself more coffee. "We need some positive energy here. Where are you going shopping, Sarah?"

"I think probably to—"

"We're going to Bloomies, of course. Then, I don't know. I guess I'm hoping Bloomies will be enough." Silvia seemed to have everything under control.

Sarah cringed. "Oh, not too expensive, okay?"

"Bloomies is perfect. Classic pieces are worth the price." Tina nodded.

As more forks came toward her plate, Julie guarded what was left of her pancakes from the others. "When is your trip again?"

"It's still a few weeks away—" Sarah was interrupted by Silvia again.

"Oh, that's right. I forgot. That's the weekend I'm moving!"

"What?" Liza leaned in.

"Yeah. I was told the ceiling in my bedroom is about to fall down, so they offered me a bigger, newly updated apartment." Silvia clapped and wiggled in her seat.

"But you live on the second floor. What was happening upstairs that would make your bedroom ceiling cave in?" Julie looked stumped.

"The guy upstairs from me worked nights, thank goodness! I came home sick one day and heard him and some woman doing God knows what up there . . . all day long. All I know is he finally moved, and they found a trampoline, an anatomically correct mannequin, and a black leather saddle in the dumpster!" Silvia muffled her mischievous laugh.

"Really? Très kink-a-a-ay!" purred Tina.

"It's actually a nicer place. It's on a higher floor, and I'll be paying the same rent . . . and better still, no loud cats fighting on this side of the building!" Silvia had often complained about many sleepless nights she spent listening to unsettling screeches outside her bedroom window.

"Oh, look over there." Tina pointed to a plainly dressed petite woman standing at the entrance to the coffee shop. "That's Mrs. Klein."

Sarah stretched her neck to look. "The lady you hate at work?"

"No! Do you ever fucking listen to me?"

"S-o-r-r-y!"

"She's the nice lady . . . the woman who was kicked out of her chair by the Viper. Isn't she so sweet? Look at her standing over there all alone waiting for a table. I'm going to go say hi. Be right back."

Before leaving the table, Tina decided to amuse herself by reviving an old argument among her friends. "Sil, I still say those cats outside your window were fucking." The girls all groaned and stared at Tina as she laughed and walked away.

"Ugh, no, they were fighting!" snapped Silvia.

"When two cats go at it, they scream and moan like they're fighting? We've told you this like a hundred times." Julie sat back and crossed her arms.

"No sir! I could hear them. I'm telling you. They sounded really angry, like they were attacking each other." Silvia cringed remembering the awful sounds.

Julie leaned in again. "Yeah, I know. That may be what it sounds like to you, but trust me, they were doing it. That's how cats—and my Uncle Jerry's girlfriend—do it. It's disgusting."

Liza almost spit out her coffee. "Your uncle? What?"

"Yeah. He stayed over once with his freak of a girlfriend. Never mind. My family doesn't like anyone to talk about that. Sorry."

Silvia sighed and rubbed her temples. "So seriously? Cats make those kinds of noises when they're—?"

"Yes!" Liza wiped her mouth and hands on her napkin. "When I was a kid, one night these two cats were going at it so loudly in the middle of the night my father jumped up, grabbed his gun, and shot it twice out the bedroom window."

"Oh my God! Your dad had a gun?" Sarah was horrified.

"Guns—more than one! The sound of the shots made the cats run away and, unfortunately, scared the shit out of my grandmother. My mother was so mad at him! She had to get up and change my grandmother's sheets and bloomers. Poor woman thought she was back in the war."

Across the coffee shop, Tina approached Mrs. Klein who welcomed her with a huge smile. "Hello Tina! It's funny to see you outside of Santé."

They chatted briefly at the door until Tina saw a small two-top open up nearby.

"Perfect timing!" Tina hip-checked a young woman trying to intercept the table and sent her flying into a busboy carrying a tray of dirty dishes. "Here we go. Right here." Tina ignored the kerfuffle and sat down for a minute with Mrs. Klein. "So what are you up to today?"

"Well, I was just going to have some coffee and then go about my errands." Mrs. Klein sat there with her hands folded gracefully. "You know, Harry and I used to do the errands together on Saturdays . . . breakfast here, and then off we went. That was a long time ago. Now it's just me, but I still love coming to this place."

"Oh." Tina noticed the faraway look in her milky white eyes and began to choke up. "What about your friends? Any family nearby?"

"Not really, dear. My sister passed about a year ago. We used to do lots of things together. You know, go shopping, play cards . . . and indulge in the occasional snort and a porno. That was fun!" She covered her mouth as she giggled while Tina's eyes widened despite the smile on her face.

"But now, I'm the last one here. My friends have all moved to Florida. They call sometimes and try to get me to move too, except . . . well, I hate to leave my house and all the memories of Harry."

"I understand. If you don't mind me saying . . . If you've got friends there, it might be fun to be with them, and you'd never have to suffer a New York winter again! That would be enough for me to go! And Harry's with you everywhere you go."

Just then a waiter came over, and Mrs. Klein ordered coffee and a donut. Tina motioned that she didn't want anything. "So, what kind of errands are on your to-do list today?"

"Well, I have to go to the grocery store, and I have to mail some letters . . . And oh, I have to stop at the pharmacy too . . . can't forget about that. And maybe pick up something for tonight."

"How 'bout a porno!" blurted out Tina, which made them both laugh. "Well, I'm off to work." Tina stood up. "Have fun today. I'll see you on Wednesday!"

Poor, lonely woman.

Back at the table, Tina grabbed her bag. "Well, my sweet bitches, I'm off." Tina tried to shake off her concern for Mrs. Klein and took the last few sips of her coffee. Before she turned to leave, the girls thanked her for starting another debate over fighting versus copulating felines. On her way out of the coffee shop, Tina looked over to wave goodbye to Mrs. Klein but found the table already empty.

Silvia and Sarah said their goodbyes and headed downtown to shop for some fancy dresses and beach attire for Sarah's upcoming trip to Florida. Fortunately, they managed to find a swimsuit that both flattered her trim figure and was attractive enough to wear in public. However, it wasn't easy.

Trying on bathing suits is dreaded by every woman on the planet (except maybe Victoria Secret models and Charlize Theron) and has been known to cause fainting, hysterical fits of rage, and seizures. Women everywhere know a day of swimsuit shopping is as horrific as finding a curly black hair in your salad! It was no surprise that searching for a swimsuit for a couple of hours sparked some discord between the two friends.

"I'm not putting that thing on!" Sarah crossed her arms.

"Why? It's so cute!" Silvia gazed at the adorable, eye-catching bikini. "Don't you want to show off your figure?"

"It's too revealing. I wouldn't be comfortable."

Silvia sighed. "Alright. Let's keep looking."

Sarah held up a beige, one-piece, mesh nightmare. "What about this one?"

"Are you serious?!" Silvia grabbed it from her hands. "It looks like something your grandmother would wear. It's so long. All you need to add is rolled down stockings and black shoes." She shoved it back on the rack.

Sarah held up another swimsuit. "Fine! What about this one?"

"Sure. I like the wide, yellow stripe! It looks like police crime scene tape!"

"Oh! Then, I don't know!" Sarah began to get teary-eyed.

"Okay, okay." Silvia took a deep breath, realizing she had to be gentler with Sarah. She reached out and held her by the shoulders. "Let's just stop for a minute. What colors do you like . . . and please, don't say brown or yellow."

"Well, I like blue and green . . . and purple."

"Great. Now, what kind of bathing suit would you feel comfortable wearing?"

"Um," stammered Sarah, "I really want a one-piece that covers me."

Silvia turned Sarah around and pointed to a spot across the store. "Please go sit over there by the mirrors and relax. I'm going to find a few swimsuits I think you might like and bring them over for you to try on, okay?"

Sarah walked over to the chairs near the dressing rooms and sat down relieved of any further responsibility. Twenty minutes later, Silvia came over holding four swimsuits she hoped would be acceptable to her.

"Here. Take these into the dressing room and try them on." She then called to the attendant, "Miss, we have four suits to try on, please."

A few minutes later Sarah stuck her head out from inside the little hallway leading to the dressing rooms. Seeing only Silvia, she emerged wearing the first rather revealing swimsuit.

"Now that looks good on you!"

"No. No way!" Sarah covered her breasts. "My boobs look like rising dough."

"Okay . . ." Silvia began to push Sarah's breasts further down into the suit.

"Stop!" Sarah giggled and raced back to her dressing room. In a few minutes, she emerged again looking very self-conscious.

"This color green makes me look like a giant pea pod." Silvia burst out laughing. Sarah was tall and lean, and she was right.

Inside the dressing room, Sarah looked at the next bathing suit and was shocked that Silvia chose such a skimpy suit. "Oh, no. I'm not wearing this. Why don't I just wear assless chaps?!"

A few older women passing by were startled by this explicit declaration. Silvia shrugged her shoulders and smiled at them. "It's okay. She's a pole dancer from Texas."

When Sarah came out of the dressing room the next time, Silvia was pleasantly surprised. This bathing suit fit her flawlessly. It was colorful and form-fitting while still covering all her girlie parts.

"I love it! You look great. Do you love it?"

"I think so . . ." Sarah grinned.

"It's so cute! You look so good in that. Here, look at yourself." Silvia positioned Sarah directly in front of the mirror and spun her around. "See? Gorgeous! It's just perfect for you!"

"Yes. I love it!" Sarah hugged Silvia and went inside the dressing room to change.

That really was adorable. Sylvia giggled to herself. "Sarah, take your time. I'll be right back!" Then she ran to grab the same one in her size.

After their successful albeit lengthy bathing suit quest, the girls were now on the hunt for a cocktail dress. Sarah became overwhelmed while looking at the vast selection, so once again Silvia took the lead. Within fifteen minutes, she presented several dresses to Sarah which she tried on and modeled now more confidently in front of the mirror. Silvia examined the fit of each one and asked her questions about comfortability and preference.

"Cross your arms. Is there enough room in the bust? Wait, no." Silvia shook her head at the plain, boxy, calf-length dress. "This one is kind of boring. Go try on the one with the open back."

"No, I don't think I like that one. It shows too much, and I'll get cold."

"You'll be in Florida!"

"They have air conditioning, you know!"

"Never mind." Silvia stood outside the dressing rooms pacing and massaging her sore neck.

After trying on two more unflattering candidates, Sarah modeled a slightly fitted, black dress with tiny sparkles and a flared hem.

"Oh, I love this one!" Silvia smiled at her pretty friend.

"Really? I like this one too." Sarah began spinning around in front of the mirror. "I feel like a *hotsy totsy*," she said, stealing a word from Liza. "Isn't it a little short?"

"Not at all. It lands right at your knee." She crossed her arms. "Do you want to look like you're going to a cocktail party or to the Home for Frustrated Virgins and Lonely Old Maids?"

"Cocktail party."

Thank you, Jesus, we have a winner!

Chapter 5

WITH LOTS GOING ON FOR everyone, it had been a while since the girls were all able to meet at Liza's. Tonight, Silvia was looking forward to having cocktails and relaxing with her friends. Once she arrived and retched into Little Bucket, she grabbed a water and a martini—a lovely complement to tonight's menu of smoked salmon and shrimp.

"Why is it you vomit so much?" Tina loved provoking her friends.

"It's not really vomit. I just get motion sickness. I told you that." Silvia took a few sips of cold water while wiggling out of her blazer and kicking off her shoes.

The girls began happily gobbling up their delicious meals, which made Liza smile with culinary pride as she watched them from the giant shoe. This evening she wore a snake-print caftan, matching head scarf, and laced-up sandals.

"I've missed you girls! How are we tonight? Everyone doing good?"

"Yes." Julie wiped the corner of her mouth. "Silvia, you're moving soon, right?"

"Oh yeah, do you need help moving?" Tina delicately balanced her plate on her lap.

Silvia nodded and took a big bite of her shrimp.

"Are you all ready for your trip, Sarah?" Julie smiled.

"I think so. My dear friend, Sil, helped me find the perfect bathing suit and some beautiful outfits, so I think I'm good to go."

"Excellent!" Liza clapped her hands. "You're going to have a ball. I feel something big is going to happen. I'm a bit psychic, you know."

Julie touched Silvia's leg. "That was so nice of you, Sil. Did you say you needed some help with the move?"

"I do, if you're not too busy. It should be just some lightweight, personal things like my clothes and shoes . . . stuff like that and maybe some unpacking if you have time. The building manager has arranged for some men to move my furniture and anything heavy."

Julie's big eyes grew wider. "Big strong men! Sure, I'll help." Everyone giggled at her interminable quest for love.

"Well, I'm sure I have to work." Tina leaned back on the couch.

Sarah became annoyed and stopped eating. "Then why did you just ask her if she needed help?" Her stern voice matched the serious black suit and starched shirt and tie she wore.

"I was curious." Tina grinned wickedly further enraging Sarah.

"Why don't you and your flying monkeys go and continue your search for the ruby slippers!"

While the two women exchanged words, Julie moved closer to Silvia. "Can I ask you something? Do you . . . Have you ever gone on any of those dating sites?"

"Well, no. Why? Have you?"

"Yes, I know it's probably stupid, but I just can't meet a decent guy and—"

"That's for sure! I mean, internet dating isn't a bad idea. You just have to be careful . . . a lotta weirdos out there." Silvia was concerned about her naïve friend. "You watch *Dateline*, right? They always have shows about women getting killed by crazed internet stalkers."

"Yeah, I know. Thanks for reminding me." Julie rolled her eyes. "I just uploaded my profile a month ago, and I already met a cute guy from Queens. He seems nice, and by his photo he looks like he's in good shape. He's Italian . . . and a general contractor."

"Oh, look at that, an Italian contractor." Silvia giggled. "Is his name Mario?"

"No!" Julie laughed and swatted at Silvia. "We've had a few really nice conversations, and he finally asked me out for coffee and a walk in the park on Sunday. I think I wanna go, then again—"

"Hold on. That's actually a good idea. A lot of guys use those dating sites for quick hook-ups." Silvia paused. "Sunday, really? Well, it's supposed to be a nice day. Sounds good to me." Julie was dying to meet her new man, so she grabbed her phone and eagerly tapped out a text message.

"Thank you, Sil, and please don't tell the rest of the girls—at least not until I'm engaged, okay?"

"I won't. Text me where you'll be going and his contact . . . Actually, text me all the information, just in case you go missing. Can't be too careful. You don't want to be featured on *Dateline*."

From across the room, Liza perked up and poured herself another drink. "So, how's Mary Louise, Sarah? She still riding you like a Grand Canyon mule?"

"She sure is!" Sarah turned to face the group while removing her jacket and shoes. "Listen to this. This week she told me to organize a department meeting. She said she wanted me to review some vital procedures with some of the staff who probably weren't kissing her ass enough. So I set it all up. I got approval for a light lunch to be delivered, wrote down the issues she wanted addressed, put a PowerPoint presentation together, and found a conference room. Boom! Done! So what does she do?"

"Oh, no! What?" Silvia held her breath.

"She strolls in right before the meeting begins, asks me for my presentation materials, and tells me to take a seat! Can you believe that? She made me sit right in front and watch her run the meeting." Sarah ripped off her tie and untucked her shirt. "It was my meeting!"

"That's so mean! It would have been more humane to make you watch Adam Sandler's awful movie, *Jack and Jill,* again." Liza looked dazed. "What was he thinking?"

"Liza . . . focus! That woman is such a bitch!" Tina gulped down the rest of her martini. "So what did you do?"

"What could I do? I sat there watching her ugly puss face up there making all of my points and taking credit for the whole thing afterwards with Mr. Casey!"

Silvia banged her hand on the table. "Sarah, you need to find another job. Now."

"Okay. Here's what you do." Liza stood up with her hands on her hips like a cowboy and spoke with a southern accent. "You get in her face and tell her you're handing out lollipops and ass-whoopins, and you're all out of lollipops!"

Liza's ridiculous imitation made everyone laugh. "It'll be okay. In the end, we all have to deal with the consequences of our actions. The universe will make it right."

Tina stood up and discreetly motioned for Sarah to follow her over to the window. For a moment there was silence.

"Hey, I'm free on Saturday." Silvia looked around the group. "Anyone want to go to that big flea market near the old tire factory?"

"You mean the Grand Bazaar? That's a good idea!" Liza clapped and bounced in her seat.

Tina turned away from her private conversation with Sarah for a moment and giggled. "I have to work, but if you see any broken chairs or old ladders, please grab one for me."

"Very funny! There's lots of good stuff there. Sometimes you can find some terrific bargains." Liza loved her treasure hunting, but Tina never understood the attraction.

"Yeah, last time I bought an old broken clock and a crate!" Silvia laughed as she indulged Tina, who understood her point.

Liza swatted at Silvia. "Shut up. You did not! You love to go—"

"I know, I'm just kidding." Silvia chuckled. "Sarah, are you coming?"

Sarah sat back down among the pillows. "Sure, why not? I haven't been to a flea market in ages. Sounds fun"

"Julie, you coming?" Julie shook her head.

"Okay," Tina smiled. "So while I'm at work, you guys have fun elbow deep in someone else's painful memories and trash no one really wants!"

"What a ball buster!"

At ten o'clock on Saturday, Silvia, Liza, and Sarah met up at the entrance to the Grand Bazaar. It was a lovely spring day—perfect for exploring and enjoying the company of friends. Silvia and Liza, both dressed in ankle-length jeans and flat shoes, each brought a rolling cart to transport all their special finds. Sarah only wore a backpack over an oversized sweatshirt to carry her purchases.

The Grand Bazaar was New York's oldest and largest flea market and had been attracting locals and tourists for many years. Silvia and Liza had been there many times and were familiar with some of the vendors. They also knew how to spot quality items, negotiate a low price, and the best food peddlers. They had gone to the flea market today in search of specific items, while Sarah was happy to roam around and follow her fancy.

"Girls, I'm looking for some funny props I can use in my act, so if you see something that would be good, let me know."

"I'm looking for some kind of small table for my front hall." Silvia beamed at Liza as they began their exciting adventure.

The girls slowly made their way down the first aisle. Silvia and Liza turned their heads from side to side checking out the items on the tables from a distance as Sarah trailed behind them zigzagging to every booth on both sides.

Within minutes, Liza stopped at a tent selling menswear and accessories. "Girls, come look at these."

Silvia immediately knew what caught Liza's eye. "You love the hats, right?" She began picking through the pile with Liza.

"This one is brown felt and has a feather in it. Here is a top hat—gotta get that. Oh, look at this one!" Liza held up a red ball cap with a giant ear on each side.

"Oh my God!" Silvia chuckled. "With that one you could tell a joke about how men never listen when women talk!"

"What'd you say?" Liza laughed while wearing the cap. She gathered her favorite ones and purchased the bunch for half of what they were asking.

Sarah finally caught up with them, and the girls continued their stroll. Soon they spotted a table featuring lots of gaudy jewelry. Though Liza was looking at the items for props, Sarah was interested in necklaces to wear to work. She found two lovely, simpler pieces with small gemstones and working clasps.

Silvia leaned over to examine the pieces. "Sarah, I love those. How did you find them among all this other stuff?"

"I don't know. I found them at the far end of the table."

"You got the radar, lucky duck!" Liza patted Sarah on the back.

Sarah turned to the seller. "How much?"

"How's two for twenty?"

"Sure!" Sarah happily paid for the items and put them in her backpack.

Liza shrugged her shoulders and whispered to Silvia. "She didn't even negotiate."

Silvia shrugged. "But look how happy she is!"

"Fine. If paying full price makes a person happy, who am I . . ." Liza walked away shaking her head.

The trio continued to the end of the aisle and then turned into the next. This row had larger tents offering furniture and household gadgets. With nothing jumping out at Liza, she walked ahead of the girls until Silvia called her over to a booth she had just passed.

"Liza, do you like that?" Silvia pointed to a small entryway table. "I was looking for a place to drop my keys, phone, gloves . . . and look at this." Attached to the side of the table was a slot large enough to hold an umbrella. "Cool, huh?"

Silvia turned to the owner. "I see you have fifty dollars on this. Can you do twenty?"

"I can do thirty."

"How about twenty-five cash?" Silvia held out her money, and the dealer accepted.

"See Sarah, that's how it's done!"

"I get it now." Sarah nodded, as Silvia and Liza smiled at their new protégé.

The girls didn't find anything else of interest further down, so they switched to an aisle that showcased a variety of smaller items—everything from old books to crazy holiday decorations.

"Liza, come look." Silvia found a booth that had lots of small noisemakers and musical instruments. "How about some of these for your show?"

When Liza walked over, her mouth fell open. "These are perfect!" She darted over to a table in the rear and selected a tambourine and a small horn with a squeezable black bulb on it. She also took a triangle and a conductor's baton off a shelf.

"Oh my God! This stuff is awesome!" Sarah shrieked. "Hey, look at this tuba!"

Silvia laughed. "You're gonna hurt yourself!"

Liza approached the owner. "I'd like to bundle these if I could. I'll give you forty for the pile?"

"Can't do that," he said. Liza stared back at the man and said nothing.

"Be right back." He walked over to his wife who nodded after whispering to her husband.

"Okay, we can do that."

It was now after one o'clock, and the girls realized they were hungry. They made their way over to the row of food vendors and each chose something different to eat. Silvia picked at a risotto ball, Liza munched on some fried chicken, and Sarah made them both jealous by enjoying coffee and a piece of cheesecake. After their bellies were full, they headed slowly toward the exit while continuing to check out the merchandise along the way.

"Oh well, it's too bad we didn't get something for Tina," murmured Liza, which suddenly gave the wickedly grinning trio a whole new objective. Silvia wandered over by the trash and in just minutes came running back with the perfect gift to give their wise-cracking friend.

"Look at this!" She held up a big, old plastic doll whose ratty clothing and gouged face made her look like the kind in scary movies. "Let's get it!" She was impressed by her own wicked idea.

"Oh, she'll die!" Liza laughed just thinking about the look on Tina's face.

Sarah examined the doll. "I can't wait to give it to her!"

As the girls continued along toward the exit, Silvia and Liza took one last look around in case they might have missed something. Sarah walked more or less all over the place, including in the back where the trucks were parked. Soon Silvia and Liza realized they lost track of Sarah. As they came to an aisle at the edge of the flea market, off in the distance they could see Sarah talking to a few men and petting a small dog. Sarah saw her friends and waved, then shook hands with one of the men and walked toward them carrying the little animal.

"What are you doing?" Silvia shook her head.

"The guy gave me this dog!" Sarah was excited as she held the small, wiggly puppy. "Isn't he cute? He said he didn't want him and was just gonna leave him here, so I had to take him."

Liza and Silvia stood back a bit. "How do you know the dog isn't sick or infested with fleas?"

"He's fine." Sarah kissed and cuddled the sweet dog.

"Please take him to the vet immediately, Sarah." Liza carefully began to pet the sweet pup on his head. "What's his name?"

"Whiskey Sour." The girls stared at her. "Well, that's his name. Why should I change it?"

The girls were hesitant but had to admit the dog was adorable. He was a brown and copper-colored mixed breed with a black spot on his nose and large furry ears and tail.

"How are you gonna take care of him? You work all day?" Silvia knew Sarah's boss was strict about her leaving the office.

"I live near my job, so at lunch I'll go home and walk him." Sarah giggled. "And starting Monday I'm going to take my whole friggin' lunch hour!"

"Good for you!" Silvia finally reached out and petted the friendly little dog who immediately started licking her hand. "So . . . Whiskey Sour, huh? He sure is a cutie!"

Liza shook her head and laughed. "Okay, then. Welcome Whisky Sour!"

"Hey girls!" Liza started toward the exit. "Let's find a bar with a patio. All of a sudden, I want a drink!"

"See?" Sarah laughed. "He fits right in!"

Chapter 6

TINA WORKED ON SATURDAY AND was asked to come in again on Sunday. Managers often had to work six days in a row, but a seven-day work week was very unusual. The schedule was crammed with appointments all day, so the owner requested a full staff that day, including herself. Her name was Dominique "Niki" LaFontaine.

Niki was a tall, gorgeous French woman with long, light brown hair and an accent that could make a list of medical side effects sound sexy. She married into a family descending from French royalty, had two children—a boy and a girl—and a nanny. She always dressed impeccably and sported a stunning yellow diamond ring that could be seen from space. She had a brownstone on Park Avenue, homes in France, California, and in the Hamptons, and, contrary to the spoiled, rich stereotype, she was a genuinely nice person. It was clear that Santé was more a pet project and a labor of love than a necessary income making venture.

Tina got along very well with her boss. She admired Niki and knew she was appreciated for working hard and taking care of the especially "difficult" clients, graciously saving her from any unpleasantness. Niki often gave her monetary bonuses and tickets to shows as rewards for her excellent work.

When she first began working at Santé, Tina told Niki she dreamed of one day owning a salon of her own. Niki loved her devotion to her work and her determination to learn every nuance involved in running a successful business. She often took her aside to explain the financial side of the beauty biz and show her how to make the best deals with the vendors and marketers. Tina took in every bit of knowledge shared by Niki and became her right hand in no time.

Today seemed to be going smoothly until Tina heard a commotion coming from the Hair Creations section. She hurried through the large French doors to investigate so Niki wouldn't be disturbed in her office upstairs.

"Stacey," Tina called to the hairdresser. "What's going on?"

In front of Stacey sat an irate redheaded woman wearing a striking aqua blue suit and fine jewelry. Upon hearing Tina's voice, she spun around in her chair and pointed at the stylist. "Do you see what she did to my hair?"

Ugh, thought Tina. It was Mrs. Rossi. The woman was a bona fide bully and a huge boozer. She reminded everyone of a nasty, drunken Lucille Ball.

"Mrs. Rossi. How nice to see you again." Tina smiled. "Why don't you like your hair? I think it looks stunning."

"Stunning? Ha! I told this one," she said, tipping her head toward Stacey, "I have to attend a benefit tonight for underprivileged children, an organization for which my husband is the chairman, and I needed extra special attention to my hair. So what does she do? She constructs this limp, unimaginative mound at the back of my head! I look like a waitress at the Waverly Diner! You want I should put on an apron and jump behind the counter?" Her words came out a bit garbled, probably as a result of whatever Tina was smelling on her breath.

"Okay, well, let's see." Tina examined drunk Lucy's alleged mound then turned her attention to the stylist.

"Stacey, why don't you go and get Mrs. Rossi a glass of champagne while I take care of this." Tina winked at Stacey as she spoke. This was a secret signal known only to the staff to bring their top-quality, non-alcoholic champagne substitute. Niki had a policy of not serving alcohol to clients who appeared drunk. Heavily intoxicated clients couldn't taste the difference anyway.

"Now, let me ask you something, Mrs. Rossi." Tina turned her chair around again to face the mirror. "What are you wearing this evening?"

"I'll be wearing a lovely, emerald-colored Balenciaga gown with gold embellishments and crystal beading." Drunk Lucy boasted about her outfit with slurred words.

"H-m-m-m, sounds lovely." Tina swept a bit more of her hair up, teased and pinned it in the back. "Let me see what else I can do. I'll be right back." As she began to walk away, Stacey showed up with the glass of fake champagne, which Tina took out of her hands.

"Here, Mrs. Rossi. Enjoy some champagne while Stacey works on this a bit more, and I'll be right back." Before leaving, Tina turned to Stacey and whispered, "Just lift the crown here, and blend it into the . . . mound while I'm gone."

Tina took a quick walk around the spa looking for some inspiration on how to fix drunk Lucy's big ugly head. Suddenly she spotted the perfect accessories. With the foyer full of waiting clientele, she made her way unnoticed over to two giant-sized flower arrangements near the front doors. Mixed in the largest plant, she spotted some branches with gold flecks just begging for their freedom. She selected a couple of the shiniest ones and hurried to her office. There, she cut them down and shaped them into perfectly pointed hair accessories.

"Look what I have for you, Mrs. Rossi . . . new and hot from Paris," she said in a sing-song-y voice. "It's the newest thing. In fact, Niki might kill me for bringing them out already."

"Oh really?" Lucy's face lit up looking at the unique French baubles Tina held up. "What will you do with them?"

"Just watch." Tina arranged several of them throughout the now teased up hairdo. She inserted them delicately in just the right spots, added some super hold hairspray, and watched in the mirror as Lucy's sour expression transformed into delight. Stacey took one look and hurried away, unable to stifle her giggling.

"Oh, my goodness. They look incredible!" Drunk Lucy was stunned. "That's so much better! Where—"

Tina spun her chair around to see the back. "I told you, it's a new French trend . . . and I believe you're our first guest to have them. They're by 'Rameuax,' and they're spectacular, don't you think?" She smiled knowing that word in French meant twigs and branches.

"It's lovely. My hair now complements my dress perfectly. Thank you, um . . . what's your name again?" Drunk Lucy's memory wasn't very reliable, or maybe it was that the names of those she viewed beneath her weren't worth remembering.

"Tina. I'm the manager here, and it's my pleasure."

Tina turned and walked back toward her office. Looking to her right, she spotted Niki standing on the staircase and leaning casually up against the Nail Salon wall. Evidently, she had watched the whole scene play out.

"What?" mouthed Tina, shrugging her shoulders at an obviously impressed Niki. They both broke into wide smiles appreciating the ruse that had just taken place. Niki then formed prayer hands and bowed to Tina in gratitude before shaking her head and walking back upstairs.

It was turning out to be a beautiful spring day. Julie picked out a nice daytime outfit for her first date. She wore a lovely white flouncy blouse over tapered beige pants with cute dress flats and a small brown satchel draped across her torso.

At one o'clock she left her apartment and headed to Central Park. She was supposed to meet her date, Michael Ricci, at the reservoir, and then the two would grab a coffee and take a walk. Before leaving, she reviewed her date's profile picture one more time and made sure she had his cell phone number saved in her phone in case there was a mix-up in meeting spots.

Julie wanted to arrive first so she could look around and get comfortable with her surroundings. When she got near there, she found the area bustling. As she made her way through the throngs of people enjoying an exceptionally gorgeous day in the park, she could see Michael off in the distance. *He's here already.* Her heart began beating in her chest, and she began to sweat. As she slowly made her way toward him, his image increased in size, and her smile increased in delight. He was dressed in loose jeans, a tight, white tee and a light bomber-style jacket. *He's really cute.* Finally, with just a short distance between them, he turned in her direction and waved.

"Julie?" He was surprised to see she was there already. Before she got too close, he shoved a large portion of a cheeseburger into his backpack. He hadn't eaten breakfast and was hoping to scoff down a burger before their date. Unfortunately, she was early. *What woman is ever early?*

"Hello!" He wiped his face on a napkin as they approached one another.

Julie smiled. "Hi, Michael! Have you been waiting long?"

"No." He tossed a piece of gum in his mouth. "Just got here a few minutes ago. Good to finally meet you in person."

As they wandered down the path in front of them, they talked about their weekend plans and discussed the interests each of them had listed on their profiles. She liked movies, baseball, the beach, and dogs. He liked softball, dogs, the outdoors, and craft beers. After they walked about a half mile or so, they spotted a coffee vendor.

Michael smiled and motioned toward the cart. "Coffee?"

"Of course!" beamed Julie.

They reviewed the posted flavors of coffees offered by the vendor and each got a cup of their favorite blend. As they resumed their stroll they discussed movies, music, and television shows, and asked each other some poignant questions such as "Do you like Elvis," "Have you ever seen a UFO?" and "Are you grossed out by people with webbed feet?" After a while, they came upon a lovely, unoccupied bench under a beautiful tree.

"Shall we sit for a minute?" Michael walked toward the bench.

"Sure. This is such a nice spot. We got lucky."

They sat quietly under the large American elm and enjoyed the gentle breeze and people-watching until their tranquil respite was interrupted by the sounds of barking dogs playing off in the distance.

"Look at them!" Michael pointed toward a field. "They're having so much fun, huh?"

"Yeah!" *Please God, let them stay away.*

"I love dogs. I don't have one right now though because my land-lord doesn't allow pets." He shrugged.

Uh-oh, thought Julie. Everyone at work told her to make sure she wrote "Loves Dogs" on her dating profile because guys like dogs. However, nothing could have been further from the truth. She had been petrified of dogs ever since a group of them chased her up a tree in Union City, New Jersey, when she was a child.

When she was ten years old, she was walking through an empty baseball field when a horde of wild dogs came rushing in her direc-tion, barking and growling and jumping all over one another. As she scrambled to look for a place to escape the stampede, she could see only the open field and one lone tree standing close by. With no other recourse, she climbed up the tree only seconds before the melee gathered beneath her. She ended up sitting on a strong low branch for almost an hour, crying and waiting for the rambunctious pack to leave the base of the tree, but they never did. Finally, a nice old woman found her and shooed away the dogs. She helped her down from the tree, comforted her, and walked her home. After that experience, Julie never got over her fear of dogs.

"If I remember correctly, you wrote you love dogs in your profile, right?" Julie was jolted out of her dazed state.

She smiled. "Oh yes, of course! And cats. I love cats too."

"Yeah, cats are okay, but dogs are the best. I had two growing up and miss having a dog now."

"I know. They're just so . . ." she stammered, "sweet and lovable."

A few minutes later, another couple came along and sat down on the bench. The bench itself was big enough, so Michael moved closer to Julie while sliding his backpack along the ground and set-tling it between their feet. Suddenly, she got a whiff of food.

"Wow. There must be a hamburger vendor nearby. Smell that?"

"Uh, not really." Michael suddenly remembered the cheeseburger he had hidden in his bag. As Julie was about to ask if he was hungry, she was interrupted by a lively cheer from Michael. "Hey, look at this guy coming with all those dogs. Isn't that great?"

She turned and saw a man walking an eager pack of dogs heading right toward them. These weren't the dogs that had been playing in the field. No. These savage animals were a variety of different breeds and sizes on loose leashes, panting and clambering to get ahead of one another, and threatening all the innocent people trying to enjoy a day in the park. Her heart began to race.

"I think he's got about six or seven of them! You know, if I knew I could make a good living walking dogs, I would do it! Wouldn't that be fun?"

"Sure." Julie's eyes widened as the dogs got closer by the minute.

"Here they come!" Michael kneeled on the ground in front of the bench, waving them toward him and calling to them in a baby-like voice. "Hi guys! Hey doggies! Come here. Come over here!" And come they did!

Six dogs pulling on their leashes scrambled towards Michael, excited by his sweet shouts and welcoming hands. They were anxious to meet their newest admirer, hoping to be petted and loved, and wanting to return that love with wet kisses and pawing.

The furry mob arrived and pushed Michael back onto the bench, then vied for a spot on his lap to lick his face. Soon their attention was distracted by the smell of the burger he shoved inside his backpack earlier. They turned and began burying their wet noses in everything in search of the delicious treat they believed must have been hidden for their amusement. Excited by the game, they were relentlessly looking for the culinary treasure they loved—beef!

As the dogs got a bit out of control, Michael reached into his backpack on the ground and pulled out a clump of the cheeseburger. Now all six dogs began aggressively competing for this small scrap of food by drooling, yelping, and jumping over one another while the dog walker stared at his phone. Sitting in the midst of their squealing, open mouths, Julie became overwhelmed with the same incredible fear she experienced years before as a child.

Believing she would be mauled to death, she unleashed a scream that surpassed Jamie Lee Curtis's shriek in *Halloween* and burst into tears that shot almost straight out of her eyes! With nothing to use as a weapon, she began waving her hands wildly, desperately trying to free herself from this animal gang bang. Feeling as though an attack was imminent, she stood up and began jumping up and down as though she were barefoot on a hot plate. Finally, she ran frantically away from the bench, taking refuge behind a tall, wide tree about thirty-five feet away.

Now safe, Julie fell to the ground crying, her clothes covered in dirty paw marks and sticky dog spit and rivers of mascara streaming down her face. When she eventually calmed down, she looked up from behind the tree and saw Michael and the dogs (and even the dog walker) looking at her, stunned and slightly amused at the sight they had just witnessed. Filthy and embarrassed, she jumped up again and ran across the park, looking back only once. She had left her date standing there, alone now, in utter shock and disbelief and with a really funny story to tell his friends.

Chapter 7

NONE OF THE GIRLS WERE available this week for dinner at Liza's. Silvia was packing up her apartment and putting in long hours at work. Tina was busy running the spa while Niki was away. Sarah was obsessing about her upcoming trip to Florida, and Julie had not left the house since the attack of the rabid dogs (the story got worse each time she told it). Liza had no plans either, so she decided to spend a long overdue weekend with her friend, Thomas.

At around six o'clock on Thursday night, Liza arrived at the exquisite Upper West Side apartment Thomas shared with his boyfriend, Trevor. The two made quite the power couple. Thomas was a very successful intellectual property lawyer, and Trevor was an affluent stock analyst who worked on Wall Street.

Thomas lit some candles, opened a bottle of Masseto red wine, and turned on the gas fireplace—all the things Liza loved.

"You're the best! I feel so fancy!" Liza quickly made herself comfortable in Thomas's uptown world and remembered how much she loved spending time with her beloved friend.

"M-m-m. This wine is delicious! You have to let me know what this is so I can get a bottle for myself." Liza put her empty glass down and stretched out in front of the fireplace on the lovely, hand-woven Moroccan rug.

Thomas smiled. "I doubt you would spend three hundred dollars on wine for yourself, so I'll send you a bottle." Liza screamed with delight and jumped up to help herself to another glassful.

"Hey, I want to show you some new suits I bought . . . come see." Thomas led Liza to his gorgeous mid-century styled bedroom complete with two giant walk-in closets and a lovely crystal chandelier. He opened the doors to his closet and turned on the light.

"Here they are. Aren't they fabulous?"

"Oh my God! Italian?" She touched the exquisite, top quality material.

"Yes! And over here . . . Look at the shoes I bought."

"Oh my God! This leather is incredible!" Liza smelled it and rubbed it against her skin. She knew he had great taste. When they were in public, the handsome Thomas was often mistaken for a model.

"Now look over here at Trevor's things." He opened the other closet door.

"His clothes are nice too!" She flipped through the wooden hangers.

"Yes, but he just buys them off the rack. The sad repercussions of growing up in Jersey, I suppose. I keep telling him to go to the tailor, but he refuses. Fine with me." He then pointed to his boy-friend's belts.

"But aren't these wonderful? I steal one whenever I can!" He giggled.

"His shoes aren't as nice as yours though."

"I know. He says he refuses to spend a lot of money on things that may come into contact with trash, spit, or dog shit!"

Liza nodded. "It's true though. Do you know how many tears I've shed over ruined shoes?"

"I know but, my God. We're not hillbillies!"

When the two returned to the great room, Liza relaxed, and Thomas called his friends to confirm their plans for the evening. After that, he prepared a little supper for the two of them. He served a light supper of bruschetta and Tuscan white bean soup—the handsome attorney was also an incredible chef. After eating, Liza retreated to the guest room and took a quick nap and a hot bath.

At around ten, the two headed out for some fun. They went to meet some of Thomas's friends at Rory's Bar for Ten-Thirty Trivia. Rory's was a popular gay bar that held various early evening events before turning into a dance club at midnight. Thomas and his friends often visited the nearby bar for its light cuisine and friendly atmosphere.

Minutes after they were seated, Rico, Marcus, Carmen, and James arrived. They were all hard-working, intelligent professionals who enjoyed having fun together. Liza was already acquainted with these good friends of Thomas, so the gang all hugged and kissed upon seeing each other again. The group settled in at a big, round high-top and got ready for game night. They picked a name for their team, passed in an official entry form, and retrieved a buzzer from the night's host, DJ Judy, who was dressed as a flamboyant version of Judy Garland in the *Wizard of Oz*.

After the waiter delivered their first round of drinks, the group raised their glasses and toasted to their team name. "To the Funny Ladies!" they shouted, proudly paying homage to Barbra Streisand's movie. The group then prepared for the game by discussing possible trivia questions and answers until game time.

At precisely ten-thirty, DJ Judy, a theater performer and drag queen, began her musical introduction which was always based on her character for the night. Tonight, she played "Somewhere over the Rainbow," sung by Judy Garland while waving at the players and the bar patrons in attendance. The place was packed with some tourists and newcomers, but most of the crowd consisted of excited regulars and their friends.

"Welcome to Rory's Ten-Thirty Trivia!" exclaimed DJ Judy. The crowd applauded and screamed with delight.

"Wow, I see we have a great crowd tonight! Joining us is . . . Grace Jones over there. Brava, darling!" The crowd clapped, and "Grace Jones" took a bow. "I also see Liza Minnelli sitting over there in the corner. Hi Liza!" The doppelganger for Liza Minnelli stood up and waved as again the crowd applauded. "And I think I see Cher. Is that you, Cher?" she asked. "Cher" stood up, flipped her long black hair back, licked her lips, and waved. "And oh, here's a surprise. I think I see Richard Simmons. Is that Richard Simmons over there?" DJ Judy paused. "Oh, no, that's just Eugene our bar-back. Hi Eugene!" The crowd laughed and clapped for Eugene, who took a bow and waved.

"I love her!" Liza clapped wildly.

"I know." Marcus nodded. "She's the best. We come here a lot, and she's always hysterical. Just wait 'til she gets going!"

"Is she always Judy Garland?"

"Mostly, but she has some other favorites too." James thought for a moment. "She dressed as Liza Minelli once or twice."

"Oh, and Cher," said Carmen.

Thomas scratched his head. "Wasn't she also Little Bo Peep?"

"That was for the Halloween party." James rolled his eyes. "And it was Little *Blow* Peep!" Everyone giggled.

"Oh, by the way," Liza leaned closer to Thomas. "Is Trevor meeting us tonight?"

Thomas reacted indifferently as he moved his chair nearer to the table. "He's out of town again, but even if he were in New York, he never comes to these things. He hates this stuff."

"Really?" She pressed him for more. "He hates having fun with friends?"

"I know, right? I love him and everything, but he has this snobby side to him . . . thinks he's too rich and prominent to hang out with my friends . . . these lovely people. I call him 'Mr. Big Stuff' sometimes. He thinks nights like this are undignified and ridiculous." He waved his hands as though he could erase the unpleasant words hanging in the air.

She patted him on the back. "Oh, that's too bad. I'm sorry."

"And it's not fair because I go everywhere with him . . . to all kinds of functions and sports events sponsored by his firm." He closed his eyes and shook his head.

Liza felt badly for bringing up such a touchy subject. "Well, at least we know how wonderful it is to keep in touch with your close friends. Forget about him. We'll have fun tonight!"

"I know." Thomas hugged her. "That's why you're here!"

DJ Judy resumed her opening remarks. "Okay everyone. Here we go!" The game was about to begin and Liza squealed with excitement.

"Tonight we have the following five teams competing for the grand prize of five hundred dollars. They are: the Broadway Babies, South Beach Queens, Funny Ladies, Gypsies Tramps and Thieves or GT&T, and Bette's Eyes." The crowd clapped and cheered for their favorite teams. DJ Judy continued by reviewing the rules of the game.

"Listen up, please. Here's how we play the game. When a question is asked, the first team to buzz in gets to answer the question. If their answer is wrong, buzzers need to be hit again in order to answer the question. And please, no shouting out answers from anyone but the contestants, okay? You maniacs at the bar control yourselves!" Everyone laughed.

"Alright! Here we go. First question: What was the name of the man Marilyn Monroe married at age sixteen?" Several buzzers were pushed, and the Funny Ladies won the chance to answer.

Thomas jumped up. "James Dougherty!"

"That is correct!" said DJ Judy. The crowd applauded and started singing, "*And it seems to me you lived your life . . . like a candle in the wind . . . never knowing who to cling to . . . when the rain set in . . .*"

"Very nice folks, but you're no Elton John!" DJ Judy giggled as the singing waned. "Next question: In what movie did Bette Davis play a girl battling an inoperable brain tumor? She was credited with one of the best dying scenes—" A few teams hit their buzzers, but Liza's team was too late.

"Yes, it was *Dark Victory*," DJ Judy confirmed, "and GT&T wins that round." The crowd applauded and began singing "Bette Davis Eyes" by Kim Carnes. The singing, however, quickly died out.

"That was fucking pathetic!" DJ Judy scolded. "Does anyone know the lyrics except for the words 'Bette Davis eyes'? No shit! This is what you sounded like: da da la la da la fa la Bette Davis eyes!" Everyone chuckled at their lackluster interpretation and clapped for their hostess.

"Okay. Here we go. Next question: Who is credited with dressing Cher in her most iconic outfits?" All the buzzers were pushed, but the Funny Ladies were first.

"Bob Mackie!" Liza shouted. The crowd cheered her correct answer, then stood up and started singing, "*If I could turn back time . . . If I could find a way . . . I'd take back those words that hurt you . . . And you'd stay . . .*"

The waiter came by and had to yell over the jubilant crowd to be heard. "Another round of the same?" Liza nodded rather than shouting back, then listened for the next question.

"Okay, let's settle down . . . You're killing me! Cher, darling, I'm so sorry. They're horrible!" joked DJ Judy. "Okay, okay. Next question: Who played Batman in the 1997 movie *Batman & Robin*?" Several buzzers sounded, and DJ Judy announced the winner.

"The Broadway Babies are correct. It was George Clooney!" At the mention of his name, the crowd began to chant, "*Clooney, Clooney, Clooney . . .*" for about two minutes until finally, they got tired.

"I know . . ." DJ Judy made a purring sound. "He's delicious. Clooney is fair game for all of us, right! Everyone loves George!" She pretended to blow George Clooney a kiss and then continued with the game.

"Okay, everyone. Next question: He debuted his glam, androgynous alter ego Ziggy Stardust in the early 1970s—" All the buzzers were slammed, and the Funny Ladies came in first.

Marcus yelled, "David Bowie!" DJ Judy hit a button on the console and the crowd sang along with the music that began to play. "*Let's dance . . . Put on your red shoes and dance the blues. Let's dance . . . to the song they're playin' on the radio. Let's sway . . . while color lights up your face. Let's sway . . . sway through the crowd to an empty space . . .*"

More than halfway through the game, DJ Judy announced the two highest scoring teams were the Funny Ladies and the Broadway Babies. They happened to be sitting at tables next to one another, so there was a fun rivalry going on between the two teams. Each table bought the other a round of drinks after answering a question correctly, and soon there were only a few questions left before the end of the game.

"Ready?" DJ Judy held her hand to her ear.

"Yes!" screamed the crowd.

"Next question: What actress's signature song was called "Falling in Love Again" and first appeared in a 1930s movie?"

Liza hit the buzzer first. "Marlene Dietrich!"

DJ Judy confirmed her correct answer, which prompted the crowd to sing, "*Falling in love again . . . never wanted to . . . what am I to do? Can't help it . . .*"

"Oh my God! This is so much fun!" Liza screamed as she and Thomas rocked back and forth in their chairs.

"I know, I love it here!" Thomas smiled and grabbed her hand.

DJ Judy waited for the crowd to finish. She leaned on her elbows and rested her head on her hands. "I have to say . . . Wow! You people have to have the worst fucking voices I ever heard! You suck!"

DJ Judy jumped up and pointed at everyone, and the crowd laughed and yelled back at her. "No, I mean it. You should all get your cover charges back and spend it on fucking voice lessons!" The crowd loved it when she teased them.

"Okay." DJ Judy was still giggling. "Listen carefully because this next question may be tricky. Here it is: In 1949, the musical, *Gentlemen Prefer Blondes,* opened on Broadway and starred what actress?" DJ Judy shrieked at the riotous response to her question as all of the players went crazy slamming their buzzers—one contestant even knocked a woman off her chair.

The Broadway Babies buzzed in first. "Carol Channing!" they shouted, and everyone began singing, "*A kiss on the hand . . . May be quite continental . . . But diamonds are a girl's best friend . . .*"

"Why did I ask that question?" DJ Judy shook her head. "My fault. I should have known . . . Carol Channing! What the fuck was I thinking?" After a while, everyone finished singing and began waving their fingers around in the air, and she was happy to indulge them.

"Now's your chance, Eugene—grab all the diamond rings! Oh, and by the way, for those who are curious, my finger is an eight and I like square stones!" Everyone chuckled as DJ Judy held up her giant left hand.

"Okay, here's the next question: Who starred in this 1969 American musical film about a matchmaker based on the 1964 Broadway production of the same name and was directed by Gene—?

Every buzzer was slammed, but the Funny Ladies were first. "Barbra Streisand!" shouted Thomas.

As soon as her name was mentioned, the crowd went wild. "*Hello, Dolly, I said hello Dolly . . . It's so nice to have you back where you belong . . . You're lookin' swell, Dolly, I can tell Dolly . . . You're still glowin', you're still crowin', . . . you're still goin' strong . . .*"

DJ Judy swayed side to side as everyone in the bar sang this crowd favorite. When they finished, they clapped for themselves and turned to her for more.

"Thank you!" DJ Judy finally got to move on. "That was much better! Okay, we have two questions remaining before we announce the champion. Good luck to both teams!"

As the audience waited for the next question, DJ Judy stared at the game card in front of her. All of a sudden, she yelled "Madonna!" and hit a button triggering the song "Like a Virgin." The crowd screamed and immediately sang along. "*Hoo, like a virgin . . . Touched for the very first time . . . Like a virgin . . . When your heart beats . . .*

Next to mine . . ." She laughed as the crowd sang and danced around the tables.

"Tricked you fuckers!" DJ Judy danced along with them in her booth. The crowd continued until she stopped the music and took some deep breaths.

"Oh my! I can't move like that anymore. I'm done! Alright all you sexy people . . . let's relax!" DJ Judy motioned for everyone to calm down. Liza and her friends wiped their faces with napkins after having worked up a sweat from dancing.

"Okay, shut the hell up!" DJ Judy jokingly scolded the crowd. "Ha, ha, ha! Okay. Here's the next question: What was the name of the man who ran a gas station brothel in Hollywood after World War II?" No buzzers went off, so a hint was given. "A gas station—male brothel. This story was featured in a Netflix film called *Hollywood?*"

Two buzzers sounded and the Broadway Babies answered. "Scotty Bowers!"

"I can't stand this!" Thomas was nervous. "Hey everybody, we have to jump on this next question, so hit the buzzer fast no matter what."

"Wow!" said DJ Judy. "That was a hard one. Who said that?" The crowd laughed and booed DJ Judy for her obvious remark. "Okay, I'm sorry. I've been a bad girl. I think I need a spanking!" The crowd squealed and banged on the tables as the hostess roared.

"Okay. We gotta get serious now. Everyone, the score is tied, and the next answer will reveal the winner of the five hundred dollar prize. Is everyone ready?" The crowd screamed, "Yes!" Then the room got quiet as the contestants readied to slam their buzzers.

"Okay. This could be another tricky one . . . Or it might not!" DJ Judy laughed. "Here is the last question: She went to Erasmus Hall High School and graduated at only sixteen—"

Thomas hit the buzzer immediately. "Barbra Streisand!"

The crowd cheered and clapped, and DJ Judy made her final announcement. "The Funny Ladies are the winners! Come and get your prize money, you lucky bitches! I love you all. Good night everyone!"

House music began playing immediately triggering the bar's transformation into a dance club. The lights were dimmed, the tables were quickly moved off to the sides by the staff, and the exchange of patrons began—game players exiting and club goers entering.

Liza shrieked and grabbed her unfinished drink from the table before it was shoved out of the way. Thomas ran to get the prize money while his friends moved to the center of the room and began jumping around to the music. The Broadway Babies came over and joined them for a celebration. When he got back, Thomas flashed the wad of cash.

"Drinks for everyone!" He stopped a waiter and ordered more drinks for his friends and the runners up as well.

The two groups chatted until the drinks were delivered. Thomas held up his glass and giggled. "Here's to DJ Judy who always ends the night with a Barbra Streisand question!"

Chapter 8

ON SATURDAY MORNING JULIE ARRIVED at Silvia's apartment by nine o'clock to help her relocate to the fourth floor. The workmen were already moving Silvia's furniture to her new apartment while she got her clothing and other personal items together.

"Hey, you made it!" Silvia welcomed her friend into her cardboard box nightmare. "I really appreciate your help. Thank you so much."

"Sure. What can I do?"

"Well, you can grab any bags or boxes that are closed and start taking them upstairs. There are two elevators. The workmen are using the freight elevator to move the furniture, so you can use the one at the front of the building."

"So where's the new apartment?" Julie started to gather a few bags.

"Up on four . . . apartment 404. Just follow the enchanting aroma of sweaty men!"

The move itself took about two hours, and after some repositioning of furniture Silvia ordered a pizza for them to eat while they put away some of her things.

"How do you think Sarah's doing in Florida?" Julie opened some boxes while Silvia stacked the shelves with books and picture frames.

"I don't know. I hope she's okay. She seemed happy with the outfits we got for the trip, so I think that made her feel a little better. Funny . . . you'd think it would be easy for Sarah to find a bathing suit. She has that long, slim body, ya know? But she's kind of old-fashioned and so modest. She turned down quite a few good choices. I felt like I was dressing an Amish woman!" Silvia giggled.

"Well, she is from Pennsylvania! You know, I think that awful Mary Louise is slowly chipping away at her self-esteem."

"I wouldn't be surprised. You know, every time that woman's name is mentioned I picture her tied to a chair with duct tape over her mouth!" The girls laughed.

"And did you see Liza's face when Tina mentioned giving Sarah some designer cosmetics? God, she loves free swag! Anyway, Tina gave her a make-up lesson before she left. That must have made her feel good. I'm sure she'll call if she's having trouble, right?"

Silvia finished with the shelves and sat on the couch. "You never know with her. Sometimes Sarah calls all upset and dramatic, desperate for help . . ." she continued in a Southern accent, "and sometimes she just goes and hides like a long tail cat in a room full of rocking chairs!"

In Florida Sarah was attending her first training session which was due to conclude around noon. As she looked around the large conference room, she sized up some of the attendees. *She looks like an executive. That guy has no clue. She's not so hot.* Soon, her attention was drawn to a rather rowdy group of good-looking men sitting in the back rows.

Obnoxious old frat boys!

As the conference came to an end, it was announced that cocktails and hors d'oeuvres would be served by the pool promptly at two o'clock. Sarah made her way to the exit to go upstairs and change clothes but saw a huge crowd waiting to get on the elevators. With time to kill, she decided to have a quick drink in the lobby restaurant.

As soon as she sat down at the beautiful mahogany bar, a handsome, tanned, broad-shouldered bartender appeared before her. "Hello. What can I get for you?"

Taken aback, Sarah giggled. "What do you recommend?" Her voice was high and squeaky.

He's a god, she thought. *He's Zeus.*

"Well, my specialty is a Long Island iced tea. How does that sound?"

This time, Sarah tried to answer in her sexiest voice. "Perfect. I'm from New York." She was hoping Zeus would make the connection between her home and the drink name.

"Really . . ." Zeus was smiling. He already knew most of the people attending the conference were from New York.

"Oh, right." Her face turned red in response to his playful sarcasm.

Zeus came back shortly with her cocktail and left her with a wink. She sat and sipped the tall, cold, expertly made drink. After a while, Zeus came by her side of the bar again.

"My God, this is delicious!" She was hoping to start a conversation with him.

"Another?" Zeus grabbed some clean glasses from under the bar. Sarah nodded and smiled, but he was off again.

Soon Zeus delivered her second drink. "So, are you enjoying your trip? Have you been here before?" He leaned casually on the bar and showed off his gleaming white smile.

"Yes, I love Florida." She moved in closer toward him. "The seminar is okay. A lot of the information is familiar to me though. I guess I'll have more free time than I thought." Without taking the bait, Zeus raised his eyebrows and nodded, but then went on to serve another customer.

Damn!

As Sarah enjoyed her second drink, she began feeling relaxed and content. *This is just what I needed.* Soon she noticed the lobby was nearly empty and decided to head upstairs to her room. She saw that Zeus was busy, so she left the amount due (plus a huge tip) on the bar and called out, "Thank you!" as she proceeded out of the restaurant.

"Have a good rest of the day!" He waved and watched her walk toward the elevators.

I wish they had more of those in Canarsie.

Once upstairs, Sarah took out the chic, by-the-pool ensemble that Silvia helped her put together. Before dressing, she decided to put on some instant self-tanner. Her skin was so white from being in New York City all winter it reminded her of the bluish color of a dead body on *Law and Order.* After applying the cream and watching it transform her skin into a nice bronze, she combed her hair, applied light make-up, and put on her new swimsuit and cover-up. Next, she strapped on glittery new wedges, grabbed her new straw hat, and loaded up her beach bag.

The pool area was crowded, but there was some space and a few empty chairs at the far end of the pool in the shade. *Perfect.* She walked slowly through the maze of chairs toward the other end of the pool. *Made it,* she thought, pleased she had not tripped and embarrassed herself in front of strangers. She found a chair in the shade facing out toward the pool. She put her towels down, fixed herself comfortably on the chair, and placed her bag beside her. A few people in that area looked over and greeted her to which she responded back politely.

A moment later, a young waiter came by and asked if she would like a drink. "We are serving complimentary rum punch, but feel free to order whatever you want."

"Thank you." Sarah was feeling very amenable after already consuming two strong drinks. "I'll try the rum punch."

He's cute, but he's no Zeus.

Her eyes followed the waiter as he made his way over to an outside patio that included a straw covered hut with a sign that read "Tiki Bar." After he disappeared from her sightline, she spotted the rambunctious group of men she had seen at the back of the conference room. They were all huddled together telling jokes, laughing loudly, and high-fiving each other about every seven minutes. She sighed deeply and looked up at the blue sky, ready to enjoy this beautiful day. Soon, however, she found that even in the shade it was hot. She heard someone say the temperature was ninety-one degrees. *That pool looks so refreshing!*

As her drink came, so did two women who took the last two empty chairs located next to her.

"Hello," said a friendly, upbeat woman wearing a large-brimmed pink sunhat. "Are you with the conference?" Sarah noticed the New York accent immediately.

"Hello. Yes, I am. I'm Sarah Green."

"Hi. We are too. I'm Helen, and this is Marie." Marie nodded at her while tucking towels into the sides of her chair.

As they got to know one another, Sarah learned that Helen was Sarah's age, but her grayish hair made her look quite a bit older. She was a little overweight but had a sweet face and a kind way about her. Marie was younger than Helen and had a gruff exterior and an impatient manner.

"Did you happen to see Gary, the bartender, inside the restaurant?" Helen swooned.

Sarah giggled. "I think I know just who you mean. He's gorgeous!"

"He's okay." Marie rolled her eyes. "My old boyfriend was just as hot."

Yeah, right. Sarah smiled at Marie. *This one's gonna be a pain in the ass.*

The women continued to chat about where they were from and what they did at work, and each gave their opinions about the conference.

"Kind of boring, I'd say," said Marie. "Didn't really learn anything I didn't already know . . . a big waste of my time."

Helen nodded. "Yeah, I guess, but I'll describe it as exciting and very informative when I get back to the office. I have to make them think these trips are worth it so they'll keep sending me, right?"

"Especially the ones held in Florida!" Sarah giggled and fanned herself with her hat.

The conversation continued intermittently, and soon the crowd in the pool seemed to lessen a bit. However, the rowdy Frat Boys were still carrying on at the Tiki Bar. After sitting in her chair for a while, Sarah found herself sweltering in the humidity.

She looked over at her new friends. "Anyone up for a swim?" Marie shook her head.

"No thanks, I'm fine here." Helen waved at her. "You go ahead, honey. We'll watch your things."

Sarah stood up and readied herself: fix cleavage, pull bathing suit out of butt crack, make sure cha-cha is covered. *Ready*, she thought. She walked over to the edge of the pool and could already feel the sun burning her skin. As she looked around she spotted the diving board at the other end of the pool. She hadn't jumped off a diving board in years. *Screw it,* she thought. *I'm doing this!*

She made her way again through the clusters of chairs and finally found herself at the foot of the diving board. It wasn't very high, and there was plenty of room in the pool to dive in and swim all the way to the far end. As she took her place on the edge, she felt lots of eyes on her. She looked to her right and saw the Frat Boys watching her. *Oh shit,* she thought, but she was too hot to turn back. *One, two, three, go!*

Sarah dove gracefully into the pool. Immediately, she felt invigorated by the cool, clear water and was relieved that she didn't do a belly flop in front of everybody. She came up, took a big breath of air, and swam the backstroke toward the other end of the pool. To her surprise, the Frat Boys were clapping and high-fiving each other. Her strokes were confident, and she beamed with pride at her stellar performance. She stopped in front of where her chair was and floated there, balancing herself with her elbows on the lower rim of the pool wall facing the cheering, whistle-blowing, drunken idiots. Savoring the rare attention, she smiled and waved back at the men.

A moment later, Marie came over to the edge of the pool and leaned down to Sarah before walking over to the bar. "Hey Esther Williams! Your top is down and your tits are exposed! Better cover up before this place gets raided!"

Sarah looked down and saw her two unrestrained, white headlights glowing and floating above the water for all the world to see—including the Frat Boys at the bar! *Fuck!* She quickly turned around toward the pool wall and grabbed at her suit. After that, the ovation ceased and the vulgarities followed.

"Nice tits!"

"Wo-o-o! Shake 'em baby!"

"Come over here and see what you did to me!"

Finally, a man sitting near Sarah spoke up. "Hey, knock it off and grow up!"

Once Helen heard the commotion, she jumped up with a towel and hurried over to help Sarah get out of the pool. Off in the distance, Marie could be seen laughing as she stood waiting for a drink at the Tiki Bar.

"Oh God, I'm so embarrassed!" Sarah wrapped the large towel around herself. "This shit always happens to me! Just when I think something is going well, I fuck it up. I'm completely humiliated. I wanna die," she whimpered. "God, just strike me down dead!"

Helen turned and placed her body between Sarah and the glaring eyes from the bar. "You're not supposed to say things like that! Pooh, pooh, pooh! It's bad luck! You have to spit three times now to banish the evil eye."

"Bad luck! I wanna die!" Sarah sat down on her chair and hurried to put on her straw hat and sunglasses as though doing so would conceal her identity.

"Pooh, pooh, pooh!" Helen grabbed her by the hand. "Stop saying that!"

Marie returned from the bar with her cocktail. "Oh, so dramatic! It's just boobs. Get over yourself."

"Those idiots will calm down soon. You'll see." Helen took her seat next to Sarah, and within minutes, it turned out she was right. Just like that, the fuss was over. The imbeciles at the bar stopped harassing her, and the crowd at the pool had returned to their own. After one brief, scandalous moment, her life returned to anonymity.

"See I told you." Helen slapped her hands together. "All done."

"Feel better, ya baby?" Marie laughed cruelly. "I don't know why you got so upset. After all, you're far from a supermodel! How long could their fascination with you have lasted?"

Back in New York, Silvia and Julie had just about finished organizing Silvia's apartment. It was almost half past five in the evening, when Silvia suddenly remembered something.

"Oh crap! I've got a priest coming at six o'clock."

Julie looked up. "You what?"

"Yeah, a priest is coming over. Every time I move, I like to have my place blessed. It makes me feel safe. But look," she motioned, "I forgot all about this. My crucifix is broken." She gently touched the statuette of Jesus on the crucifix. "See? His feet are still nailed here at the bottom," she pointed out, "but the little nail holding his hands has fallen out here at the top. I've got to fix this before Father Donohue shows up."

"Where did you get that?" Julie examined the old wooden cross. "It's very big."

"I know, but I love it. I've had it my whole life . . . since I was born. What should I do?"

"Well, got any little nails?" Julie looked around the apartment.

"Ew!" Silvia shook her hands wildly.

"What?"

"I really don't feel comfortable re-nailing Jesus to the cross!"

"Oh, right." Julie covered her giggles with her hand. "Well then, how about Super Glue? Got any of that?"

"Yes, I do! I just put it away under the sink, actually." Silvia grabbed the glue and set the crucifix down on the kitchen table.

She carefully put a few drops of Super Glue on the back of Jesus's hands and held them tightly to the wood for about a minute.

"You're a genius."

"Well, the Vatican does consult me about these things." The girls laughed.

Silvia released her grip on the crucifix. "It looks like it's holding, but I better let it sit here and dry for a while before I put it up."

The two girls continued putting Silvia's things away, and at six o'clock the doorbell rang.

"That's Father Donohue!" Silvia jumped up. "Could you please buzz him up while I hang the crucifix over my bed?"

"Sure." Julie headed toward the door, and Silvia raced to her bedroom.

Father Donohue said hello as he entered the apartment. He was a short, stocky man who always reminded Silvia of the angel that was sent to George Bailey in the movie *It's a Wonderful Life*. After some small talk, the priest asked Silvia to tell him exactly what she wanted him to do.

"Well, Father, I'd like to have my apartment blessed. I just moved in, and it would be of great comfort to me."

"Sure." He began praying immediately. "In the name of the Father—"

"Oh Father, I'm sorry," she said. "Can we please do this in front of the crucifix over my bed?"

The group moved into the bedroom and stood facing the crucifix on the wall. After blessing themselves, they closed their eyes and folded their hands at their waists while the priest began his blessing of the home.

"May this home always be filled with God's love. May this home be a place of peace during the night and day. May it be a haven of—" In the middle of the priest's prayer, an unsettling "whoosh" sound startled the trio.

The priest abruptly stopped praying and opened his eyes. There was the crucifix still hanging on the wall, however, Jesus had suddenly changed position. Though his feet were still nailed at the bottom of the crucifix, his hands had let go at the top, causing him to spin around and stop in an upside-down position.

"Jesus Christ!" exclaimed the petrified priest.

"Oh my God!" Silvia jumped back and gasped.

"This is awesome!" Julie fell to the floor laughing.

The priest's eyes darted around the possibly possessed apartment. "What the hell is going on in this place?"

"No, Father . . . It's not . . . Please let me explain." Silvia smiled awkwardly. "My crucifix was broken, and I just superglued it back together. See . . ." She pointed at the statuette. "Jesus's hands were glued back on here at the top just a few minutes ago . . . before you arrived, but I probably didn't use enough glue, so it didn't hold."

"Almighty Father! Do you know what an upside-down crucifix means, young lady?" The priest was clutching his chest with one hand and the silver cross hanging around his neck with the other.

Julie looked at the priest with a furrowed brow and pursed lips. "What?"

"Some say it means nothing," he wailed, "but I know different. I've been a priest for nearly forty years, and I've seen it all! Believe me! That . . . that . . . upside-down crucifix is a symbol of the occult . . . demonic interference!" The priest began backing out of the room.

"You mean Satan?" Julie giggled at the absurd implication.

Father Donohue stopped in his tracks and stared at her. "What do you know of the ruler of the devils?"

"Nothing. Nothing at all!"

"No, Father, really," Silvia once again motioned for him to look at the crucifix. "I just superglued the hands on right before you got here, and it didn't hold. That's all that happened. It's really nothing! Please continue with the blessing."

"Oh Lord and Savior help me!" The priest sat on the edge of her bed, rubbing his bald head and trying to pull himself together. After a few minutes of grumbling, the still trembling priest stood up.

"Fine." He began the blessing again, speeding through the prayer like an announcer at a racetrack.

"May all who dwell in this place feel God's presence. May the Lord bless you and keep you. May he shine his face upon you. May the Lord lift up his countenance to you and give you everlasting peace . . . In the name of the Father, Son, and the Holy Spirit. Amen."

When he was done, Father Donohue stared at the crucifix on the wall for a moment, looking for any subsequent change in Jesus's position. Seeing no further movement, he accepted Silvia's donation check and sprinted for the door, murmuring, "God Almighty, I need a fuckin' drink."

In Florida, Sarah had recovered from her embarrassing afternoon and was about ready to face her first evening at the conference. Tonight was the welcome party for the attendees, and she was dressed in her new, beautiful, black cocktail dress with matching bag and shoes. She styled her hair up for a change, which made her feel polished, elegant, and hopefully, unrecognizable. After one last look in the mirror, she left her room, took the elevator to the mezzanine level, and headed toward the large ballroom.

Just inside the doors she found the sign-in table where she was given a badge with her name on it. The ballroom was plain, but there was music playing and a private bar at the front. As she looked around, she noticed a lot of the other women were dressed in business attire, but held her head high, feeling unusually calm and confident in what she was wearing. After making her way over to the bar, she ordered a martini because the wine selection offered there was abysmal. Thankfully, there was no sign of the Frat Boys or the ladies she met at the pool. Though she liked Helen, she didn't want to spend any more time with Marie. She took her drink and turned to walk away as a woman approached the bar and greeted her.

"Hello. I see you got a martini. That looks good."

Sarah smiled. "I hope so. Are you enjoying the conference so far?"

"It sure beats the weather back home, right? Didn't feel like May when I left. Hi, I'm Joanna Carlson." She shook Sarah's hand. "I run the Department of Banking and Insurance in New York." She was tall, blonde, and in great shape. Her exquisitely accessorized outfit and confidence immediately intimidated Sarah. However, her kind smile and sense of humor put Sarah at ease.

"I'm Sarah Green. I work at the Department of Records . . . for now anyway."

"Oh, interesting. I know someone there. Her name is Mary Louise Janssen." Hearing her name almost made Sarah throw up. *Oh my God! What if she tells Mary Louise what I just said?*

"Actually, I work with Mary Louise." Sarah smiled nervously. "What a small world."

"It sure is . . . and now I completely understand why you said 'for now.'" Joanna touched her on the shoulder and grinned.

"Oh, thank God!" Sarah let out a sigh of relief. The women continued talking and walked over to an empty round table to sit down.

Joanna got comfortable in her seat. "Yeah, I feel for you. I worked with her many years ago. She is . . . well, she's something. She's always been bossy and very insecure. Hey, does she still wear those big shoes?"

"Yes—those ugly fucking shoes!" Sarah banged on the table. "But they do match that ever-so-charming personality! The woman is brutal. Even our department head won't deal with her."

"Well, it doesn't sound like she's changed much." Joanna seemed to understand Sarah's plight.

"She's probably jealous of you, ya know." The comment startled Sarah.

Mary Louise is jealous of me.

"That woman doesn't play well with others. She sees any attractive, capable woman as a threat." Joanna shrugged. "So if you're unhappy, why don't you quit?"

"Actually, I'm really not sure why I'm still there."

"Let me ask you something. You appear to be very capable and professional. Will your performance reviews—I assume they're done by the department head—be flattering and rate you well?"

"Oh, yes!" Sarah nodded. "Casey loves me. He's fair, and he's a great guy."

"Oh, yes. I know Mr. Casey. Good." Joanna fished around in her handbag. "Here, take my card and check us out. If you decide you want to make a change, give me a call."

The women continued to get to know one another at the table, although it was a bit difficult given the loud, thumping music and shouts from the people on the dance floor. Soon a waiter came by and they ordered two more martinis.

In the middle of a story, Joanna suddenly stopped and pointed across the floor. "Oh my God, look at that woman coming out of the ladies' room. She's got a length of toilet paper stuck to her shoe! I like to tell people when that happens. So many people don't say anything and I always feel badly." She started to get out of her chair when Sarah stopped her.

Across the room, she could see Helen walking toward the bar followed by Marie in the midst of an embarrassing moment.

"Don't bother." Sarah smiled widely.

"Why not?"

"Because what you're actually witnessing is karma hard at work!"

"What do you mean?" Joanna tilted her head.

Sarah looked up and giggled. "Just trust me."

After a few more drinks, the women decided to move over closer to the DJ stand. Some of the people on the dance floor were already pretty intoxicated and actively seeking others to join them. Sarah turned and spotted a wildly enthusiastic dancer. "Hey, look at that tall, creepy guy in the black shirt and jeans."

"Ew! He gives the term 'boogie man' a whole new meaning!"

Sarah covered her mouth. "Oh my God! The woman he was dancing with just walked off the dance floor!"

Joanna laughed. "Not stopping him though! Look at him go all by himself!"

Finally, a song came on that both Sarah and Joanna liked, so they put their things down on a nearby table and jumped into the mix. Sarah was actually having fun! It seemed like hours before the two women took a break from dancing and sat down. Fanning herself, her eye caught sight of the clock on the wall. It was almost eleven thirty, so she told Joanna she wanted to go upstairs. Joanna nodded and smiled while blotting herself with a napkin. The women waved goodbye to the others still dancing and left the ballroom.

Once in the elevators, Sarah pressed her floor number, but Joanna didn't move.

We must be on the same floor.

When the elevator stopped, Joanna followed behind Sarah down the hallway. Finally, Sarah spoke up.

"What room are you in?"

"I'm in 1203," replied Joanna sheepishly.

Sarah laughed. "This is the 16th floor. You missed your floor, silly! Are you that drunk?"

"Oh, is it? I didn't realize." Joanna's shaky voice matched her awkward attempts at retrieving her keys from her cluttered purse. "I'm so tired. I don't know what I'm doing."

Sarah gently turned Joanna's shoulders around to face the opposite direction. "That-a-way!" she giggled, while pushing her gently down the hall toward the elevators.

"Goodnight!" she called as she unlocked her door.

Joanna didn't turn around; she just waved as she hurried back toward the elevators.

Once inside her room, Sarah felt a bit uneasy and confused as she slid into her bed and turned off the lights. *What just happened?* Within a few minutes, sleep vanquished any questions on her mind and she forgot all about it.

Chapter 9

ONCE AGAIN, SILVIA FOUND HERSELF riding in a taxi from her job to Liza's apartment for a girls' Thursday night dinner. It felt like years since they all had been together and she was anxious to get there. Traffic was horrific tonight, and she became more impatient and nauseated by the minute.

"Oh my God!"

"Nothing we can do," the driver called over the somewhat loud beat emitting from his electronic fusion radio station. He looked out the window at the massive congestion. "It's not like Uber can get you there any sooner, lady."

Upon her arrival, Silvia was excited and relieved to be free from the driver's sarcasm and his awful taste in music. She paid him, flew out of the taxi, and bounded up the hallway stairs to Liza's apartment. After puking in Little Bucket and washing up, she headed into the sunroom where her friends were already indulging in steak tips and ribs.

"Sorry, I'm so late . . . Traffic. Oh, I hate this feeling." Silvia groaned and rubbed her stomach. "But that food smells delicious."

"So why are you sick all the time anyway?" Tina grinned wickedly.

"I told you. I'm not sick all the time," she snorted. "I just get motion sickness from riding in taxis."

"So then why do you—" Tina stopped in mid-sentence once she saw Silvia's face turning red.

"Girls!" Liza clapped her hands. "Behave!"

"Alright, I'll stop. Forgive me." Tina got up and grabbed a bottle of water for Silvia. "Here. Have some nice cold water. You'll feel better."

She took the bottle, held it to her forehead for a moment, and then took a few sips. "Thanks," she mumbled, as Tina winked back.

All of a sudden, Liza began clearing her throat incessantly while tilting her head toward the right side of the room. Finally, one of the girls noticed an addition to her eclectic art collection hanging on the wall behind them. It was a giant abstract painting full of colorful shapes and random line segments—a new and exciting find, according to Liza.

"So, what do you think?" Liza stood in front of the painting looking at it lovingly and pointing to it with the graceful hands of Vanna White.

"It's fucking huge!" Tina blurted out without thinking.

Julie could see nothing except a mishmash of wild designs. "It's eye-catching."

"What is it, exactly?" Sarah asked timidly.

Thank God! Silvia had been holding her comment until she could figure out what it was.

Liza stared at her newest acquisition clearly seeing the artist's intention. "It's an abstract of a woman dancing! Isn't she lovely?"

"Oh, yeah, I see it now. It's exquisite!" Tina wasn't even looking at the painting. She was too busy chewing on a juicy piece of steak.

Sarah slammed down her fork. "Must you talk with your mouth full of food?"

"Yes." Tina shoveled more food into her mouth and smiled at Sarah.

"Silvia?" Liza looked straight at her, eagerly anticipating her opinion of this new, beloved work of art.

Silvia put her plate down on the table and walked over next to Liza. She stared at the painting, leaned in and out, pursed her lips, and then turned to face Liza. "It makes me feel happy."

Liza gasped and hugged Silvia. "Me too!"

The rest of the girls glared at Silvia, hating her for having offered the perfect compliment. She smiled back smugly at her unimaginative, envious friends.

"So Sil, I've been meaning to ask you. How's your new apartment? You had some decorating to do when I left—not to mention an exorcism!" Julie laughed again at the comical ordeal.

"Oh yeah, we heard about Upside Down Jesus!" Tina smacked her leg. "That was just crazy. Talk about perfect timing."

"Oh my God," screamed Julie, "I thought the priest was going to faint!"

Silvia laughed out loud. "I thought the priest was gonna shit!"

"And have you heard any cats fighting in your—"

Sarah threw a pillow at Tina. "Not this again, Tina! Nobody pay attention to her!"

"No. It's been very quiet, but thanks for asking!"

"You know, crucifixes scare me." Liza pushed her plate away and popped a handful of red hot candies into her mouth. "I never understood how you people can look at those things. I mean, they're very unpleasant."

Tina threw the pillow back at Sarah and asked her about her trip.

"My trip was good. The weather was great. I went to the seminars and attended the events. I made some connections . . . nothing much else happened." Sarah flashed a fake smile and shrugged her shoulders. She didn't feel like getting into all the details.

Julie leaned in with her eyebrows raised. "Did you meet any interesting men?"

"Interesting? No."

Silvia winked. "Did you get any compliments on your bathing suit?"

Sarah remained stone-faced. "Yes, I was bombarded with lots of whistling and catcalling."

"Alright. You don't have to be sarcastic. I was just asking." Silvia got up to get another drink.

"Oh, I'm sorry. I'm just aggravated!" Sarah rubbed her face and leaned her head against the couch. "I had another difficult visit with my aunt and uncle. I know they're my relatives, but they're not like me. They're so—"

"Normal?" Tina grinned.

Sarah sighed. "Very funny. No, it's awful! The food is lousy and the apartment is filled with cigarette smoke! God forbid they should open a window!"

"Believe me. I can relate!" Silvia nodded and pointed at herself.

"I end up leaving there smelling like an ashtray. I have to go home and shower and wash my hair again—twice in the same day!" Sarah pulled at the ends of her hair. "After we eat microwaved dinners that my aunt pretends she cooked, she goes in the kitchen and washes the dishes. I offer to help, she says, 'No.' Then, she'll yell to my uncle, 'Do you want coffee, Bill?' and he yells back, 'I'll take the trash out in a minute!'" She paused while the girls tried to stifle their giggles.

"Sure, it's funny to you!" Sarah leaned back and crossed her arms.

Julie felt badly. "Well, how old are they?"

"They're both eighty something."

Silvia smiled wryly. "What about hearing aids? Have you shouted that suggestion to them?"

"They think they're too young. My uncle is still driving!"

"Holy shit!" Tina jumped.

Liza leaned forward. "Do they have any of their own children that you could talk to?"

"No. They're deaf, childless chimneys! I just sit there wearing my baseball hat and watching the television with the volume on sixteen!"

"Oh, poor you!" Tina turned to Sarah. "Visiting my family is no bathtub full of Jell-O either. I show up for dinner at my parents' house, and there's always a short, horny Chinese nail salon owner sitting at the table grinning at me!"

"Ladies!" Liza smiled at their unoriginal complaints. "That's family."

"Alright . . . calm down you two. Personally, I think we could all use a vacation. We could all go to Cancun. It's beautiful there!" Silvia started to get excited. "What do you all think?"

"I wish I could afford it. I'd love to get out of town." Liza sighed and put her feet up.

Silvia giggled. "I remember this one time me and a bunch of my friends from school took a trip to Cancun. We were at a nightclub one night and my friend, Karen, who had gone up to the bar alone, comes back to our table dragging a handsome Mexican guy by the hand. She was hammered and said . . ." now mimicking her drunk friend, "'This is Hola.'"

Everyone chuckled at Silvia's imitation.

"So I say, 'Really, his name is Hola?' and she says, 'Yes.' So I ask her, 'Karen, is it possible when you told him your name, he said hola?'

She says, 'Yes.' So I tell her, 'That's not his name, Karen. When you said hello, he said hello. Hola means hello in Spanish!' So she says, 'Well fuck me, I took French!'"

"Silvia, you never told me that story!" Liza laughed.

"I just remembered it. Wow, we were so young."

Julie shook her head. "Unfortunately, I don't think I can afford a trip right now."

"*These little town blues . . .*" Liza began singing in an attempt to lighten the mood.

"Hey, Frank, can you put a pin in that? Did anyone see the paper last week?" Tina put her plate in the dishwasher and then returned to the group.

"There was a bit about the charity event my client, Mrs. Rossi, attended. I think I told you guys about how I decorated her hair—"

"Oh, yes. I know what you're going to say!" Silvia knew everything about high society in New York because of her job at the *Post*.

"Okay, I figured you knew." Tina continued, "It seems a fight broke out at this charity event that was held to raise money for New York's underprivileged children, and Mrs. Rossi was smack dab in the middle of it!"

"Really?" Liza moved in closer so she could better hear and see Tina in the candlelight.

"Yes. As liquor was being thrown down the gullets of the rich, punches were being thrown near the coatroom! Evidently, two partygoers got very drunk and were caught making out . . . namely, Mr. Rossi and his firm's charity organizer!"

"Shut up!" Liza was fascinated by this juicy gossip.

"I guess Mrs. Rossi came out of the ladies' room and just happened to walk the wrong way, catching her husband and—I think her name is Virginia Carlisle—kissing and touching and . . . Well, you get the picture. Wifey, who I'm sure was blotto, went nuts and attacked them both! Long story short, the press was there, of course, and got photos of the brawl. They plastered a picture of the two women flailing at one another—"

"Yes, there was a great picture in the *Post,*" Silvia boasted.

"I heard that the claws came out. There was vulgar name calling and threats, and I think even Mr. Rossi ended up with a bruise or two! The best part about it was, even though the photos clearly showed Rossi's dress was ripped and hanging off . . ." Tina paused for a moment and laughed out loud. "Those fucking twigs I put in her hair could be seen clearly in the photo—still intact on her head! I spoke to Niki, and she was hysterical. She loved it! She told me she cut the picture out and framed it!"

The dramatic turn of events for this nasty woman made everyone happy and seemed to get Liza all fired up. While her friends continued enjoying their dinner, she got up and stumbled through the pillow pile on the floor and over to the stereo on the shelf.

"I know, let's have a little music." Liza looked through her music selection before returning to her seat on the giant shoe. As the music began, the girls jumped up and danced all around the sunroom to the *Saturday Night Fever* movie soundtrack.

Liza raised her hands over her head. "W-o-o-o! I love this music!"

"Go Liza!" Sarah clapped her hands.

"I'm the Disco Queen!"

"We haven't gone dancing in ages." Silvia was doing her best imitation of John Travolta.

"Yeah . . . since 1977 by the looks of it!" Tina mocked.

"Oh, I miss this." Julie joined Silvia by swinging her hips and pointing her finger in the air. *"Ah, ha, ha, ha, stayin' alive, stayin' alive . . . Ah, ha, ha, ha, stayin' alive . . ."*

"I've never gone dancing with you guys." Tina looked at her goofy friends. "Probably best to leave it that way!"

After dancing to a few songs, Liza began huffing and puffing so she sat down and surveyed the room. The mood was high and the girls looked as though they had enough dancing, so she walked over to the stereo and turned down the volume.

"Okay, girls. I have news! Please, sit down." Liza was still breathing heavily as were the girls who fell down around her in the center of the room.

"I shouldn't be this winded." Silvia touched her chest. "I think I need more exercise."

"Ha! That was fun!" Julie fanned herself with her napkin.

Liza clapped her hands to get everyone's attention, and then with outstretched arms announced, "Girls, I am on my way to becoming a star!" Her outfit that night included a white, batwing-sleeved blouse so when she raised her arms, she looked like an angel.

Silvia wiped the sweat from her forehead. "Really, what happened?"

"I got a gig!"

"Gig?" Tina rolled her eyes.

"Well, that's what it's called in the business," explained Liza. "See, I know I have to start small. I mean, I can't just show up at a nightclub with some jokes and say, 'Let me on stage, I'm funny.' So, I figured I'd practice my jokes on my own private audience."

"Us?" Julie's shoulders met her ears.

"No, silly. I know you girls love me and think I'm hilarious, so I had to find a more objectionable audience—people I don't know who will react honestly to my routine. People who might like to hear some funny jokes . . . for free!"

"While I agree that you need a more 'objective' audience," Silvia continued, "I'm wondering who they might be?"

"A friend of mine from the boutique set me up. I'm going to be entertaining a group of women in a shelter for being abused or recovering from addiction . . . something like that. It's called . . . wait, I have it written down here . . . The Safe Harbor Center for Domestic Violence Victims and Substance Abuse Survivors. Isn't that a great idea?"

Julie smiled. "Yes, it is." They all marveled at Liza's ingenuity and benevolence.

"Have you written anything yet?" Tina was almost afraid to ask.

"I'm not saying, but I want you all to come and sit in the back. My friend told me it would be alright. So, you're coming?" Liza blinked her eyelashes sweetly.

Sarah pulled out her calendar. "When is it?"

"Next Thursday night. Oh! That's perfect . . . even though it kind of cancels out a possible dinner together. Sorry, is that okay with you girls?"

Silvia looked at her friends. "Sure. Afterwards, we can grab something to eat."

Tina murmured to herself. "Oh, this ought to be interesting!"

Liza's first official stand-up comedy show was now on the calendar. No one knew exactly what to expect, but knowing Liza, it was guaranteed to be memorable.

The following Thursday evening, the girls headed to The Safe Harbor Center for Domestic Violence Victims and Substance Abuse Survivors for Liza's debut performance. It was a rundown building that housed more than a dozen displaced families, including some defeated-looking women and children, and a few others who appeared a bit sickly due to past drug abuse.

When the girls entered, they found the main community area on the first floor was clean and plain with random tables and chairs placed around the room. In the far corner of the room were two large couches and a stack of pillows and blankets. Two volunteers were busy moving the tables out of the way and positioning the chairs in rows of four facing the front window where a makeshift stage had been set up.

Liza arrived five minutes before showtime and made quite an entrance! She wore a leopard-print button-down jacket and black velvet pants with matching leopard-print hat and gloves.

"Hello everyone!" Liza waved at the unknown group of women.

Silvia whispered, "Tina, are those velvet pants?"

"Um, yeah . . . and it's seventy-five degrees out."

As the children were gathered and escorted upstairs to eat ice cream and watch television, Liza made her way toward the front of the large room. When everyone was seated and the girls took their spots along the back wall, the total audience consisted of about twenty-eight women. The lights were turned off and a spotlight came on. Actually, it was an old lamp sans shade Liza brought from home. She took her spot "center stage" and positioned the bulb so it highlighted her face. She took a deep breath and began with a smile while glancing down at small index cards she held in her hands.

"Hello ladies. My name is Liza Levy and I am so glad to be given the opportunity to come here tonight at . . . The Safe Harbor Center for Domestic Violence Victims and Substance Abuse Survivors. Let me just say before I start that I hope in some small way, I can bring some happiness to you all even just for a few minutes . . . a break from all your problems and cares of the day. [Pause.]

"So hi everyone! An all-women audience, great! So men, right? The bastards. [She chuckles.] What's the difference between men and pigs? Pigs don't turn into men when they drink. [She chuckles.] [No laughs.]

"Yeah, men can be real jerks. I just read a recent study that found that women who carry a little extra weight live longer than the men who mention it. [She chuckles.] [5 laughs.]

"Let's see . . . And for the moms here . . . The kids must be driving you crazy all cooped up in this small place. Too bad there wasn't a parenting handbook. You could smack them over the heads with it. [She chuckles.] [2 laughs.]

"Um . . . If you feel bad about yelling at your kids, just remember that some animal mothers eat their young—so you're not really doing that bad. [She chuckles.] [No laughs.]

"Okay. How many of you hate your bosses? [She chuckles.] The other day my boss told me to stop acting like a flamingo, so I finally had to put my foot down. [She chuckles.] [2 laughs.]

"My last boss said I have a preoccupation with vengeance . . . we'll see about that! [She chuckles.] [2 laughs.]

"And I have a lot of jokes about unemployment, which I'm sure some of you can relate to, but I don't think they're funny. They just don't work. [She chuckles.] [5 laughs.]

"Okay. Now . . . Oh, I have great friends also. Two of my friends work for the government. Most of you here, I think, are familiar with the government, right? They're supposed to help you ladies get those confidential P.O. boxes to help you avoid your crazy exes? But when you call to set it up, they say there's like a four to six week wait. No rush, right? Let's hope your stalker is a procrastinator! [She chuckles.] [No laughs.]

"Yeah . . . Stalking is when two people go for a long, romantic walk together, but only one of them knows about it. [She chuckles.] [No laughs.]

"*I recently had a run-in with a clerk at the Department of Motor Vehicles—now there's a messed up government department. The woman helping me was a real moron and looked like Tammy Fay Baker. I told her, 'Lady no amount of make-up in the world can cover up stupid.' [She chuckles.] [5 laughs.]*

"*Ah, and speaking of make-up, another friend of mine works in a salon and sells high-end beauty products to rich women. As I look around here, though, I can tell none of you are her clients. [She chuckles.] [No laughter.] Those are the women who become obsessed with plastic surgery, right? They just end up looking windblown!*

"*And speaking of addiction, I was addicted to something once . . . the hokey pokey. But thankfully, I turned myself around. [She chuckles.] [5 laughs.]*

"*And unlike some of you here, I once bought some shoes from a drug dealer. I don't know what he laced them with, but I was tripping all day. [She chuckles.] [2 Laughs.]*

"*And I heard meth can really do a number on your teeth, but I guess it doesn't matter here because there's really nothing to smile about. [She chuckles.] [No laughter.]*

Liza continued for about another fifteen minutes and received the same pathetic responses from her audience. By the end it looked as though she would be lynched. When she finally looked up at the girls in the back, she could see them wildly waving their hands for her to stop. Tina was even giving her the "sliced throat" sign with her hand.

"*Okay well, I gotta go now. [She chuckles.] So good night everyone, and I hope that in some small way I managed to lift your spirits and touched you all intimately.*"

Once Liza stepped off the platform, the girls raced to the front and got her out of there. They forgot about their dinner plans and instead headed across the street to the nearest bar they could find.

"What was that?" Sarah grabbed the sides of her head as Liza began crying into her monogrammed handkerchief.

"No, now, it's okay." Silvia shot a disparaging look at Sarah. "That's what this first show was all about . . . practicing and learning, right?"

Tina leaned in. "Touched you all intimately—do you know what that means?!"

Silvia sighed in frustration. She could see how upset Liza was and didn't think analysis and criticism from her friends at this particular moment was appropriate or helpful.

Julie touched Liza's hand and whispered, "Why did you say all those terrible things to those poor women?"

"Because my friend, you know, the one who got me the gig (the term "gig" triggered eye rolls from the girls) said to . . ." Liza paused, wiped her eyes, and then counted on her fingers, "be myself, dress nicely, and relate to your audience. And that's what I did. My jokes were about my audience."

Sarah nodded. "Oh, honey, they sure were!"

"And I was trying to be like Don Rickles!" Liza cried harder.

"Nailed it." Tina motioned to the bartender. "Shots all around!"

Chapter 10

AT THE NEXT SCHEDULED THURSDAY night dinner, the girls arrived to find Liza happily filling up plates with her famous beef stew and homemade popovers. This evening she was dressed in a long, loose gold and aqua silk top and matching wide leg trousers. The last to arrive was Silvia who, after concluding her usual gastrointestinal ritual, joined the rest of the girls hovering around the stove. Once seated in the sunroom, the girls kicked off their shoes and indulged in Liza's scrumptious dinner.

Silvia smiled. "Liza, as always . . . delicious! Your popovers are my favorite!"

"I've never had your beef stew before. It's absolutely incredible!" Julie closed her eyes and tipped her head back.

"Thank you, but the Crockpot really did most of the work. I love to spoil my girls! Eat up, everyone."

"And the place looks immaculate. How did you have time for all this? Didn't you have to work at the store today?" Silvia looked around and felt as though something was off.

"I got home early, actually. Today was my last day at the boutique. They laid me off."

"Oh, that's too bad." Julie stopped eating.

Sarah groaned. "Oh, I'm sorry."

"That sucks. I'm sorry." Silvia leaned in closer to Liza. "Do you have any leads on another job?"

"Um, I know about a couple of things. I had coffee with my friend from Con-Ed last week, and she happened to mention that her brother is opening a restaurant. I could probably call her and see if there might be something there for me. And . . . oh yeah, Thomas said he knew of a filing clerk position downtown, so I'll follow up with him later."

Liza never seemed to worry about losing or changing jobs. Her philosophy of accepting life and all that comes with it always worked for her. It also proved to be a lot easier on her stomach than Silvia's method of worrying about everything.

Silvia patted Liza's back. "Well, that's good. If I hear of anything, I'll let you know."

"Oh, and the lady downstairs is always trying to get me to join her psychic monastery."

Ministry, thought Silvia.

"Her psychic—" Tina's chin fell to her chest.

"Yes, she's a psychic and has a few women working for her doing readings and stuff. We had a conversation a while back, and when I told her I was a little psychic, she said she knew that! Can you believe it?" Liza was amazed. "So, if all else fails that might be fun."

Tina smirked. "If she's psychic, why didn't she know you were getting laid off?"

"It doesn't work that way." Liza sighed. "Sometimes if you're not . . . how do I explain it —tuned in—then you miss stuff. Anyway, I'm working on my comedy too, so I'll be fine."

"Well, with any luck, there may be an opening in the NYC records department soon!" Sarah chuckled and looked at Tina.

"I'm sure."

"You'll be fine, Liza." Julie smiled. "The falling cat always lands on its feet."

"Speaking of cats—"

Silvia glared at Tina who abruptly stopped talking and covered her mouth.

"Anyone want some coffee or tea?" Liza got up and walked over to the kitchen counter.

Silvia followed Liza with some dishes. "Hey, Tina, you know who I saw the other day? Penis Guy!"

"Really? You saw him?"

"Who? How come I don't know this?" Liza ran back over to the girls. "Who's Penis Guy? What happened?"

Tina cracked up. "I can't believe you actually recognized him!"

Liza stomped her foot for attention, and Silvia laughed as she rejoined the group. "He was there the night Thomas invited us to that office party, remember?"

"Oh yeah, I remember that, but where was I? —"

"Probably off with Thomas somewhere dancing as usual."

Julie punched a pillow. "Damn. I couldn't go that night. I can't believe I missed this . . . Penis Guy!"

Silvia made herself more comfortable among the pillows. "Tina and I were sitting at the bar, and this weird guy comes over and leans on the bar next to me. He was from Boston. He was clearly drunk, and he talked really, really fast. I could barely understand anything he said. He was all . . . 'Hello, blah, blah, blah . . . the Red Sox, blah, blah, blah . . . New York sucks.' I only talked to him for a few minutes . . . about sports, of course."

"A-a-a-h!" Sarah raised her fist. "The famous New York-Boston rivalry."

"Of course! So as I said, I could barely understand him, but he kept talking to me so I kept shaking my head and nodding at him as he rambled on . . . you know, to be polite. So, I'm barely even listening to him, when all of a sudden, I hear him say the word 'penis.'"

"Shit!" Liza crossed her arms like a disappointed child. "I can't believe I missed this!"

"Anyway, I hear him say that word, and I look at him and say, 'What did you just say?' and he looks at me and says, 'What?' So I say again, 'What did you just say to me?' and he says, 'I don't know, what did I say?' So—" Silvia and Tina laughed, both knowing what was coming next.

"So I say, 'I can hardly understand what you're saying. You talk really fast, and I'm hoping you're just drunk and not a dirty-psycho-religious freak because it sounded like you just said, 'My penis don't smell like Jesus!'"

The group erupted into hysterics.

"What?!" Sarah rolled off the couch, and Julie covered her mouth with both hands.

"I know, but that's what I thought I heard!" Silvia closed her eyes for a moment before continuing. "So, he looks at me and says, 'Why the fuck would I say that? It doesn't even make any sense.' So I say, 'I know, that's what I thought . . . Then tell me what you said?' Now, the guy's completely confused and scratching his head trying to think of what he said. Then he says, 'I know for a fact all I was talking about was sports.' So for a while he keeps muttering to himself, and all of a sudden, he turns and says, 'The last thing I remember saying to you is, 'My team is down ten this season.'"

The girls shrieked with laughter at Silvia's faux pas.

"I know! But don't they sound similar . . . especially with all the noise in a bar and his mumbling?" Silvia nodded, as the girls pointed at her while still laughing.

Tina's eyes widen. "Wow! Who's the psycho freak now?!"

"I know! I obviously misheard him. I was so embarrassed! Then he says to me, 'What kind of fucked up mind do you have?' Now, Tina and I are leaning on the bar practically crying. So we decide to go but . . . before we get up to leave, Tina leans over to him and says, 'So what does it smell like anyway!'"

Liza ran to the bathroom as the girls howled.

"I know! That was just wrong!" Tina covered her face. "Everyone knows what balls smell like!"

"Oh my God!"

Sarah shook her head again. "How did I miss that? I was there that night . . . where was I during all this?"

"I don't know . . . maybe you were with Liza." Silvia wiped her eyes.

Julie could barely speak. "And you recognized this guy on the street?"

"I think so. I only got a glance, but it looked just like him. I had just grabbed a coffee and was heading out of the coffee shop as he was entering. As we passed, we looked at each other for a moment. I don't think either of us could place our faces at the time."

"I wonder if he remembered you afterwards, like you remembered him. Ah, good times!" Tina laughed and shook her head.

Julie shrugged. "Imagine? What were the chances of you seeing him again . . . a stranger in a bar?"

"Like eight million to one!" Sarah pursed her lips and tilted her head. "Was that the party Thomas's office threw after they closed that huge deal?"

Liza sat down fanning herself with an ad she ripped from *Vogue* magazine. "Yes! It was a great party. We danced all night! Hey, I wonder if Thomas would know who he was. I'm gonna ask him."

Julie got up and sat next to Silvia. "Oh, I meant to tell you that I saw some nice first editions at the old book shop . . . the one near Thomas's office, if you're interested."

"Thanks. Right now, I'm in the process of putting up some cool art around the apartment. I also found a few copies of the first scribblings of some of my favorites, like Dorothy Parker and Zelda Fitzgerald, and I'm framing them."

"Zelda Fitzgerald, not F. Scott Fitzgerald?"

Silvia nodded. "Right. I like reading pieces by women writers, especially the first writings from those less appreciated."

"Fuckin' eh!" Tina held her fist up as a symbol of women power.

Sarah walked over to the stove and back. "No more popovers?"

Liza pouted. "I'm sorry, Sarah. Next time, I'll make more. So Sil, do you like your new apartment better than the old one?"

"Yeah. It's bigger and the layout is more open, which means I have more area to clean. Oh, I tried those Mr. Clean wipes—they work great! And I tried that Swiffer thingy on my floors too. I just love that commercial with the old couple—"

"Oh yeah, I love that commercial!" Liza clapped. "The old Swiffer couple. Love them! I gotta incorporate them into my act somehow. Funny old Jews!"

"Lee and Morty Kaufman of Long Island, New York," announced Tina. The girls looked amused.

Liza slapped her palm against her forehead. "How the hell do you know that?"

"I don't know. It's a habit. I hear a Jewish name, I pay attention."

"Oh, right." She nodded in agreement.

"And on another, more depressing note, I submitted another article this week, but I shouldn't get my hopes up because they'll probably tell me it sucks. This is just never going to happen." Silvia dropped her head.

Julie rubbed Silvia's arm. "Hey, don't say that. Sure it will."

Liza spat three times. "Pooh, pooh, pooh! You shouldn't have said that out loud! Now spit away the bad luck!"

"Not this shit again?" Tina rolled her eyes.

Silvia spat three times too. "I'm sorry. Are you happy now?" Liza nodded.

"They did that in Florida too." Sarah sat flipping through a magazine. "A lady spit like that after I told her I wanted God to strike me down dead." Everyone stared at her waiting for the rest of the story.

"Don't ask."

"Yes. Despite what anyone thinks," Liza shot Tina a dirty look, "we will all continue to banish the bad luck and only culminate positive vibes. I believe the Florida Jews were the ones who brought it over from the old country."

Sylvia winked at her. "It's 'cultivate.'"

"Maybe we should've spit three times before your last show then." Tina giggled, and Liza tilted her head in confusion at both comments.

"You know, the lady on that commercial reminds me a little of Mrs. Klein. You guys saw her at breakfast, remember? She's just so sweet and nice, but I think she's lonely. She doesn't do anything with anyone . . . says she has no friends or family left. And no one in the spa ever talks to her when she's there. I feel so badly for her." Tina closed her eyes and sighed. "Every week she gets massages and a mani/pedi, but I think she mainly comes in for the company . . . And those heartless witches keep messing with her!"

"Oh, poor thing." Sarah pictured the elderly woman's sweet face.

"I know, but I make sure the staff chats with her when they can. So the other day, Mrs. Klein got a haircut which, by the way, came out so cute! I noticed she'd been hanging around in the foyer for a while afterwards, so I went over and asked if something was wrong. She told me her ride never showed up, and she was all worried about missing her program."

"Her program!" Julie squealed. "How sweet."

"I wonder if it was *General Hospital*." Liza appeared to be talking to herself.

"Well, I needed a coffee break anyway, so I called a car and took her home because she seemed kind of upset. It wasn't very far. Her house is so big—crazy expensive real estate definitely, but a little decrepit. Poor lady probably ran out of money at some point and couldn't keep up with repairs. Anyway, when we got there, she invited me in for a cup of tea."

Julie smiled. "Well, that was nice. How was the inside?"

"Incredible! Really ornate wood carvings and those old copper ceiling tiles . . . The place must have been phenomenal in its heyday, I'm sure. We sat in the kitchen and she made us tea and told me some stories about her and Harry, her dead husband. They had a lot of fun in their younger days. I think they had a good life together. Anyway, after that, I left. I hated leaving her in that enormous place all alone, but I had to get back to work."

Silvia patted Tina's leg. "Well, you did a good thing."

"What a mitzvah! And because of that and how much we love you—" Liza smiled, looked at Silvia, and motioned with her head toward the bed.

"Oh, yeah. We bought you something a while back and keep forgetting to give it to you!" Silvia got up and reached under Liza's bed.

"Really? Why? What is it?" Tina was surprised and a little suspicious.

Everyone was excited as Silvia passed the box to Tina. "It's nothing . . . just a little something from all of us. Go ahead and open it!"

"Really? Oh, you guys!" Tina shrugged her shoulders and unwrapped the box as the girls held their breath. Soon, the paper was removed and she opened the lid. The scary doll with the broken face from the flea market stared up at her.

"What the fuck?!" Tina dropped the box and waved her hands as the girls screamed with laughter.

"What are you gonna name her?" Liza could barely get the words out before running back to the bathroom.

"How about Annabelle?" Sarah fell over laughing.

"From the flea market, right? You guys are fucking horrible people, you know that?!" Tina growled and walked away as her friends roared.

"Come back, Tina!" Silvia howled.

"Go fuck yourselves!" Tina went to get another drink.

It took a while for the group to calm down as Tina continued to rant about her sucky friends. During the fuss, Julie motioned for Silvia to come into the bathroom.

"Hey, I need a favor."

"I thought you mastered the potty." Silvia giggled. "Sorry. What's up?"

"I met another guy on the internet and he wants to go on a date."

Silvia raised her eyebrows. "You went back for more? Does he have a dog?"

"Very funny!" Julie shook her head. "And I took that off my profile."

"So what's the favor?"

"Well, he has this friend—" Julie said.

"No. No way!"

"You make it sound like radiation poisoning!"

"No—"

"Oh please, Sil," Julie begged. "I can't even imagine going on another first date after what I've been through—not without a friend with me. I'm too nervous . . . and look . . ." She opened her phone and showed Silvia a photo. "He sent me a picture of what his friend looks like. See?" Julie zipped through the photos on her cell phone. "That's them in their softball uniforms. That's my guy on the left. His name is Zack, and that's your guy. His name is Sam."

"H-m-m-m, not bad." She had to admit he was cute.

"And it's supposed to be a day date . . . the kind you recommended. They asked us to go to the zoo in the park and then maybe grab some food. Come on, it should be fun."

"Doesn't sound that horrible." *Wait, what did I just say?*

"Hey, when was the last time you went out with someone? Never mind, I know! It's been over a year. Please!" Julie kept begging her to come along.

"I don't know—" Silvia whined.

"I knew you wouldn't let me down!" Julie hugged her dependable friend.

"Stop! Send me the pictures and I'll think about it. And don't say a word to anyone about this. I want all the details about your guy and my . . . this guy, and if I decide to go, then we can plan a day. Will you let me think about it?"

"Sure. Why not?" Julie smiled from ear to ear.

Famous last words.

Chapter 11

AT THE NEXT THURSDAY NIGHT dinner, Silvia arrived a little less enthusiastic than usual. She felt nauseated, her latest article had been rejected, and she was experiencing a bit of anxiety. After hurling into Little Bucket, she cleaned up and headed into the sunroom where Liza had just served this week's feast: Chinese food from their favorite restaurant, the Imperial Palace. This evening she was dressed in a long, blue and black kimono and embroidered flat shoes.

"Score!" Silvia grinned sheepishly and sighed. "I really needed comfort food tonight. Such a day I had!"

"What's going on?" Liza handed her a plate.

Tina looked at Liza. "You know that kimono you're wearing is Japanese and not Chinese, right?" Liza's mouth fell open as she looked down at her outfit.

"I got rejected again. My article . . . for the fourth fucking time!" Silvia dumped a large spoonful of rice onto her plate but sipped some water before eating.

"I'm sorry." Sarah sat down with her plate.

Julie patted Silvia's shoulder. "It's not fair. I know how hard you work."

"No, it's fair. I'm just not good enough." Silvia was disappointed in herself and just wanted to wallow in self-pity, although she knew her friends meant well by trying to encourage her.

"That's not true." Liza moved next to Silvia. "You gotta keep at it, right? Like me and my comedy. It's going to be a lot of work. But am I giving up? No!"

"Really?" Sarah was surprised. "You're going to . . . do that again?"

"I am not giving up!" Liza motioned with her fist. "I know that show was—"

"A train wreck?" Tina smirked.

"It was my first time! How am I supposed to know everything my first time?"

Julie nodded. "Exactly. I give you so much credit for getting up there. You were so brave."

"You're right." Tina held up a newspaper that was lying on the table. "I'm sorry. Someday we're going to see an ad in the entertainment section of this paper announcing one of your shows."

"That's right! You have to be brave to get anywhere, and you're gonna make mistakes like I did." Liza leaned in closer to Silvia. "Let me ask you this, Sil. What have you been writing about?"

"Look, no offense, but I don't really want to talk about this anymore."

"Come on. Seriously, tell me."

Silvia stopped eating, licked her fingers, and sighed. "Well, you know, different things. One was about women and their struggles in the corporate world. Another was about how looking professional—you know, your appearance—inspires confidence and can lead to success —that one I got from you, Tina."

"Aw-w-w, I'm touched." Tina bowed her head.

"The third was about how pets have been scientifically proven to invigorate the elderly and help the sick get well, and this past article was about women in politics."

"There! That's the problem." Liza sat straight up. "You're not picking topics that really matter to you. You need to write about a subject that makes you an emotion investor."

"You mean 'emotionally invested.'" Silvia smiled. "Funny, that's pretty much what Bradford told me."

Sarah leaned on her elbows. "What are you really interested in telling the world? What story do you feel must be told?"

"That's exactly what I'm saying. Once you figure that out, it's going to make all the difference." Liza got up to get another drink.

"Well, you know I love your cooking!" Silvia called.

"I know you do, but you're not writing a cookbook."

Tina flipped through a few more pages of the paper and began to laugh. "Have you guys ever read any of these personal ads? I love to read them. They're hysterical. Listen to this one. 'Looking for someone to be my daddy. I love to be pounded . . .'" The girls all screamed.

"And oh my God! This one is from a man: 'I want a hairy muscular woman! Is that too much to want?' Oh, gross!" Tina shrieked. "And this one from a woman says, 'Been practicing on my pole, now all I need is yours.' People are so fucking strange!" She threw the paper back down on the table as the girls giggled and groaned in disgust.

"Now there's an idea." Sarah got up with her plate. "Julie could place an ad in the personals."

Tina scoffed. "Yeah, 'I have a Catholic school girl uniform and am looking for a bald man in a tall pointy hat with incense and a slow moving glass car—'"

"Very funny!" Julie threw a pillow at Tina.

"Oh!" Tina jumped up. "Remember I told you guys about the woman we call the Viper? Well, I just found out something interesting. The Viper used to be a stripper!"

Silvia gasped. "Oh! Are you serious?"

"A-a-a-h!" Liza shrieked, loving the sound of fresh gossip.

"Yes! I heard she was trailer park poor and worked as a stripper in a club . . . in Milwaukee! And that's where her biggest fan—now her husband—met her years ago while he was on a business trip! And guess what her stage name was . . ." Tina pointed to each of the girls.

"Cinnamon!"

"Bubbles!"

"Cherry Pie!"

"Nope. Her stage name was Blaze! I guess she wore this hot, red G-string number under a sort of fireman's outfit . . ." She stood up and danced like a stripper while everyone whistled.

Silvia was surprised. "That's actually a cool name."

"So that uppity woman was a stripper whore . . . I love it!" Liza clapped. "How did you find that out?"

"One of the massage therapists overheard her whispering to her best friend about how her husband was being threatened with exposure if he didn't fork over some serious money. She said she was upset because he didn't care if her secret got out. She said he flatly refused to pay because, after all their years of marriage and all his success, it didn't matter to him. He said his only concern had been that his mother not find out, and she's dead. She said he had until the seventeenth of this month to pay. Needless to say, her reputation and bogus pedigree will soon be shot to hell!"

Liza chuckled. "See! I told you that woman would suffer for her . . . peccadillies!"

"Peccadillos," corrected Silvia. *She's so cute.*

"More rum punch for everybody!" Tina began filling up everyone's glasses.

Julie looked at her phone. "Hey, Sarah . . . Tina just mentioned the seventeenth. Isn't your birthday coming up?"

"So what? Just makes me another year older. Look guys, don't make a big deal."

Sylvia checked her calendar too. "It's actually in a couple of weeks . . . and it's on a Thursday. Shall we go out to dinner instead of eating here? We can give Liza a break from hosting and have a little celebration."

"Can't do that." Liza looked like the cat that ate the canary, as everyone stared at her. "I have another gig!" She smiled and bit her lip.

"You what now?" Tina put her hand up to her ear as if she heard wrong. "Did you say 'gig' again?" The girls looked frightened.

"I'll have you know, I got another—" she started to say the word "gig" again but stopped abruptly. "I got another engagement at a retirement home on the Island where my grandmother's best friend lives."

"I thought your grandmother was dead." Tina gulped down her drink.

"She is, but her friend is still alive. She's like a hundred and lives on Long Island at The Happy Ending Elder Facility."

"No way! That's the name of the place?" Tina burst out laughing.

"Well, it's really The Happy Trails Elder Living Facility, but that's what I call it."

"Oh!" Tina was disappointed.

Julie grinned. "So, in two weeks, you're doing a show for old, um . . . elderly people?"

"Yes!" Liza clapped. "But I produced a different one."

"Oh, you're a producer now." Tina giggled.

Liza ignored her. "This one's better. I can't wait for you all to hear it. You're coming, right . . . my best, best, best friends in the whole world?" With her eyebrows raised, she nodded and smiled at her friends.

"Of course!" Silvia looked around at the others.

Tina shrugged and raised her empty glass. "Here's to a captive audience who will, most likely, laugh at anything because they're old and sweet and hard of hearing!"

Silvia, Julie, and Sarah met early for drinks before Liza's second show. It was Sarah's birthday, so they wanted to celebrate with her while also indulging in a little conscious sedation to prime them for later. Liza declined their invitation to join them, claiming she needed time to get "centered and prepared" for her show "like all the headliners do."

After toasting to Sarah (and a group prayer that Liza's audience didn't try to kill her), the girls took a taxi to The Happy Ending Elder Facility. When they arrived, they expected to find a gray, institution-like building where its forlorn residents had been abandoned by their families. Surprisingly, it was a cheerful, lively elder residence with lots of people and bright colors.

"Welcome!" The facility director greeted them at the door. "You must be Liza's friends."

"That must have been easy to figure out. We're the youngest ones here," murmured Sarah.

"Come on in, and please help yourselves to some refreshments." The woman pointed to a table full of soft drinks and water.

"Where's the booze?" whispered Tina. Silvia smiled and shook her head at the ridiculous question.

"Well, it would have helped the audience the last time." They both giggled.

"Please. Take a look around. All of the paintings and crafts we display are made by our residents," said the director. "As you can see we have quite a beautiful campus, and if you look down that corridor you'll find the entertainment center where Liza will be performing . . . in just about fifteen minutes. So head on in and have fun!" She smiled and hurried off to continue escorting seniors down the hallway to the show.

The girls walked around the lobby.

"Not bad, right?" Silvia admired the lovely decorations.

"Yeah. I think they have fun here." Julie pointed at the bulletin board on the wall in front of her. "Look at this. They play cards and put on plays . . . They have group walks, dances, bingo, yoga—"

"Eh." Tina shrugged her shoulders. "I won't be coming to a place like this. When I get old I'm going to sit on my ass and drive my Chinese children crazy . . . just like my Chinese mother does and her Chinese mother did . . . It's our custom!"

"Children, huh?" Sarah smiled.

"Shut up!"

As they made their way into the hall, they spotted a stage at the far end of the room. It was a good size—large enough to have a small concert or put on a play. The room was filling up, and before it got too crowded the girls took their seats along the back row.

Sarah looked around the hall. "I hope she has a microphone this time because these folks don't look as though they'll be able to hear much."

"Like I said, that may be a blessing!"

"Stop it." Silvia was nervous. *God, I hope she does well.*

The girls smiled at the sweet elderly residents coming in for the show. Within minutes they began to panic as they saw the size of the crowd growing.

Silvia reached out to the others. "I think we should hold hands and say another prayer."

"Good idea." Julie and Silvia blessed themselves.

"Holy God, please, please, please, don't let Liza suck tonight. Please! Amen."

"Couldn't have said it better myself." Tina giggled.

Julie grinned. "I hope God listens to you, Silvia. After all, you did embarrass his Son recently!" Silvia laughed out loud and quickly covered her mouth with her hand.

Tina snorted, "That may be the funniest thing said here tonight!"

After a few minutes, Liza appeared. She walked into the hall wearing a long black dress and sparkly cape matched with a feathered hat and long black gloves.

Tina's mouth fell open. "Is she wearing a cape?"

"Oh God." Silvia dropped her head into her hands.

As she walked down the long aisle toward the stage, Liza picked up on the excitement and began waving and blowing kisses to everyone she passed. Once she spotted her friends, she waved and yelled, "Hello, my girls!" and proceeded onto the stage.

"Great. Now people know we're with her." Tina sunk down in her seat.

"S-s-s-h-h. I'm so nervous." Silvia shook her hands to loosen up. It was time.

As the audience settled, Liza pushed a button on a portable CD player and music began playing throughout the hall. The song was "In the Mood" by Glenn Miller from 1939. Some of the residents began to sway and clap in their seats, while a few more agile residents got up and danced in the aisle. She took her place at the front of the stage and listened while the song played out.

Tina was watching the elders dance. "Oh God, someone's gonna break a hip."

"How many people do you think are in here?" Silvia whispered to Tina. "Fifty or sixty?"

"Does it really matter?"

Julie was more optimistic. "Isn't this exciting? There's a lot of people here."

Sarah leaned over to Silvia. "What do we do?"

"Brace yourself!"

"Go to your happy place!"

When the musical introduction finished, Liza stepped up to the microphone and began:

"Hello everyone. My name is Liza Levy and I am so glad you liked the music. Yay! [She clapped and the audience clapped with her.]

"I am happy to be here tonight to entertain all you wonderful people who, as I look around, make me feel like a child again visiting my Aunt Gussy and Uncle Bernie in Miami." [She chuckles.]

"Oh, no." Silvia sank down in her seat.

"This performance is dedicated to my Uncle Morty who just recently passed. Some of you may know him. Back in the day, he was often referred to as a 'Legend in Laundry.' Here's to you, Uncle Morty!

"Okay, well, that music was from 1939—the start of World War II. My grandfather fought in that war, but he had a big problem—he could never throw anything away . . . he died holding on to a hand grenade. [She chuckles.] [5 laughs.]

"Most people think of an old age home as a dark, dreary place where the elderly are put because they have become a burden to their families.

122

[She chuckles.] But that's not true. It's very nice here, and the staff are trained how to deal with the issues faced by their residents. They collect all the matchbooks and car keys, sew addresses into jackets, cook only soft food, and clean poopy butts! [She chuckles.] [2 laughs.]

"Still, it's unfortunate, but I've heard when left alone some old folks have mistakenly brushed their teeth with bunion cream or sprayed their hair with air freshener. [She chuckles.] [8 laughs] Some of you here may have done something similar. Looks like the woman sitting over there used hair dye as a mud mask. Don't worry, lady. It should fade in six to eight weeks! [She chuckles.] [5 laughs]

"But for those of you who don't have many family members visit, don't feel bad, there's an upside. You don't have to change out of your soiled pajamas, you can call the remote the 'clicker' without being harassed, and you can leave your teeth anywhere you want!" [She chuckles.] [8 laughs.]

"Fuck," whispered Tina. "She's doing it again!"

"Also, I would think that living in a well-run establishment such as this simplifies your finances . . . because they charge so much to live here! [She chuckles.] [5 yell "Yes!"]

"Here you don't have bills to worry about like paying Con-Ed, fixing a leaky roof, or dealing with 'customer service' from the cable company. [She uses air quotes.] They're brutal, right? [She chuckles.] Everything here is taken care of for you by the staff and, of course, the government. You can just sit back, watch the Golden Girls, and wait for those s-w-e-e-e-t Social Security checks to roll in. [She chuckles.]

"I mean, you really only have to spend your money on things like Denture Grip, Bengay, and Preparation H. [She chuckles.] [5 laughs.]

"And it seems easy to make friends here—some of which you'll have for your whole lives! [10 people laugh.]

"You know, I have great friends. I tell them, I believe that we'll be best friends until we're old and senile . . . And then, as we lose our memories, we'll be new best friends! [Laughter.]

"And your living quarters are pretty nice too. [She chuckles.] Most of you have really made it feel like home. When they were giving me a tour of the place, I noticed in some of the bachelor rooms the men have hung pictures of their favorite pin-up girls like Betty White and Angela Lansbury. [She chuckles.] [10 laughs.]

"And the ladies have made their living spaces look homey by displaying photos of children and pets . . . and themselves when they were young and hot. [She chuckles.] [5 people moan.] Their crushes back in the day were real men, like Burt Reynolds and Steve McQueen, who they dreamed would steal them away for a ride on their hogs. [She chuckles.] [10 laughs.] Lady, that means motorcycle! This is a PG rated show! [She chuckles.] [15 laughs.]

"But I noticed there are even some married couples here. While I was walking around, I heard one woman say to her husband, 'If I had poisoned you thirty years ago, I'd be out on parole by now.' [She chuckles.] Ma'am, talk to the nurses. It may not be too late! [She chuckles.] [20 laughs.]

"One thing I did learn here was how to get a sweet little 80-year-old lady to say the F word—by getting another sweet little 80-year-old lady to yell 'Bingo!' [She chuckles.] [20 laughs.]

"And don't believe it when they say that when you move into a place like this, your life is over. It doesn't have to be. Just watch the movie, Cocoon, and you'll see what I mean! [She chuckles.] [5 laughs.]

And I've been told the original Grumpy Old Men can be seen every afternoon on the sun porch! [She chuckles.] [15 laughs.]

"I think one of the secrets is to stay young at heart! Think like a teen-ager and find an orderly that will smuggle in some booze!" [She chuckles.] [10 laughs.]

Liza went on for a bit longer until finally the girls realized an end to their anguish was near.

"Anyway, my time here is about done, and I want to thank you for your attention and hospitality. As I look at your wrinkled smiles and into your milky eyes filled with knowledge and experience, my hope is that, when I'm old like you, I will get to live in a wonderful place like this—only Jewish. A place where someone like me will take the time to give the residents an experience like this one—a performance they'll be talking about for years to come! [She chuckles.] Shalom, everybody, and may God bless you all!"

As Liza took a bow, the sweet old folks clapped politely. She descended from the stage and proceeded up the aisle shaking hands with her confused and tolerant audience members. When she neared the last row, she turned to her loyal and flummoxed group of friends, whipped around in her cape and said, "See girls, I told you! I'm going to be a star!"

"Happy birthday, Sarah!" said Silvia, as the group got up and followed Liza on her descent into comedy hell.

Chapter 12

OVER THE NEXT FEW WEEKS Silvia had many deadlines. She had to finish editing two stories and was working on her own article as well. By Friday she was especially frustrated. The article she prepared for submission was finished, but even though she had edited it about a thousand times it didn't feel quite right. Finally at around three o'clock, she kissed it goodbye and emailed it to the department editor. *Que sera, sera!*

This particular article was about her mixed family and how her great-grandparents ended up settling in New York City. She thought it was an interesting story, and it was about something she was familiar with, as suggested by Mr. Bradford and her friends as well. Unfortunately, it was sent on a Friday afternoon and she knew she would be wondering all weekend if it would be accepted. Fortunately, she had agreed to go on the double date with Julie, so at least tomorrow her mind would be focused on something else.

On Saturday morning Silvia awoke and did her usual errands in the morning and then returned home to prepare for her afternoon with Julie and the guys. She decided to wear a simple beige tee under a beautiful sweater that featured bright fall colors. Brown fitted pants and cute, low boots completed her smart outfit. Her date's name was Sam Newell, and his picture showed he had a good body and a handsome face. Though she researched his name on the internet, she couldn't find any information about him other than some local amateur baseball stats.

The plan for today was for the girls to meet their dates at the entrance to the Central Park Zoo. It was a gorgeous fall day and strolling around looking at the exhibits sounded like an easy first date. There would be lots of interesting things to see and talk about and nothing awkward, unless they happened upon some animals humping. The girls took the train and arrived about ten minutes late. As they approached the designated meeting spot, they saw their dates standing with their hands in their pockets and smiles on their faces.

"Hello! So sorry we're late. Train, ya know." Julie grinned.

"Hi ladies," said Zack. "No problem, we just got here. You must be Silvia."

Silvia smiled. "Yes, I am, and you must be Sam."

"Hi. Nice to meet you." Sam shook her hand. *Very formal.*

After a brief discussion about the beautiful weather and their favorite zoo animals, they made their way inside. The guys bought the tickets, so the girls insisted on paying for ice cream along the way. Silvia felt a little uncomfortable as Sam walked along with his hands still in his pockets and his focus on the animals. However, she noticed Julie and Zack had an immediate connection. They were both smiling, and there seemed to be a sort of familiarity between them.

Zack pointed to the exhibits around him. "Did you know that this zoo houses about a hundred and fifty different species of animals?"

"No, that's incredible." Julie scanned the area.

"Yeah, they built a lot of exhibits and habitats here specifically for the animals so—I'm sorry. I have to ask . . ." Zack said suddenly. "Why don't you have a boyfriend?"

"Oh, I don't know." Julie was unprepared for such a direct question. "I guess I just keep picking the wrong guys. Oh, I'm sorry, I didn't mean—"

"I know what you meant. It's just that you're so pretty and nice and . . . Are you a jewel thief, drug dealer, consistent parking violator—?"

Julie shyly shook her head.

Zack sighed. "I seem to keep doing the same thing myself. Picking the wrong women has become some sort of a crazy hobby of mine. I think I told you already . . . I work in our family business. I'm the chief science officer at Tenney Telecommunications and a lot of women don't find that very sexy."

"What do you mean?"

"It's like they want someone who has an exciting job, like an airline pilot or a doctor or a Wall Street tycoon. I don't know. I guess a man who handles tiny equipment every day is a turn-off!" Zack laughed.

"Oh, my God!" *He's nice and has a good sense of humor!*

"But I'm me, and that's my boring job, and I'm happy with that."

"Well, good for you! I work at the IRS—a romance repellant if there ever was one!" They laughed and suddenly realized they had lagged behind Silvia and Sam, so they hurried to join their friends.

When the group got to the snow monkey habitat, Julie ran right up to the giant cage to see them. "I love these little guys!"

Zack ran up behind her. "Me too!"

At that point, Sam and Silvia made eye contact and exchanged smiles. They both seemed to have noticed how adorable Julie and

Zack were together. Shortly after leaving that exhibit, the foursome found an ice cream stand and Silvia bought a round of cones for the group.

"I see you got pistachio." Sam smiled at Silvia's choice.

"Yes, it's my favorite."

"Me too." He began feeling a bit more relaxed.

"Then why didn't you get it?" She smiled trying to be playful.

"I panicked. I figured vanilla was a safe choice in case I dropped it all over my shirt."

"That's smart." *He's shy, but funny. I can work with this.*

They continued through the zoo and saw grizzly bears and a snow leopard. They also saw walruses and sea lions at the Garden Sea Pool. Around the next turn, they came to the bird sanctuary where they saw peacocks, puffins, toucans, and macaws. Although there were also parakeets, lovebirds, and parrots, everyone's favorites were the penguins.

As they arrived at the penguin exhibit, Zack took Julie's hand. "Do you know penguins have no real enemies and aren't afraid of humans?"

"Really?" Julie smiled coyly. "I've heard that a male and a female will continue to . . . mate with each other for life. Is that true?"

"Yes. And until the baby is born the parents will take turns holding the egg between their legs to keep it warm. Now there's a guy for you . . . he even helps out with the kids!"

Silvia turned around and laughed at their conversation. "Oh, come on, you two! All this mating and egg talk is making me uncomfortable!"

Everyone laughed and the group moved along passing right by the reptile exhibit, which they all agreed was gross. They followed the trail down another hill and finally found the lion and tiger exhibits.

"Aren't they gorgeous?" Silvia marveled at the regal animals.

"They sure are!" Sam was in awe of the beautiful beasts as well. "Wouldn't you just love to be able to play with those big cats?"

"Yeah, well, I actually went into a cage once and petted a 590 pound tiger named Tessa." Silvia loved bragging about having touched a live tiger. "And she had all her claws and teeth!"

"What?!" exclaimed Sam. "How were you able to do that?"

"It was years ago in Aruba. How it works is, the trainer's there the whole time and feeds the tiger a big slab of meat a few minutes before you go in, so she isn't hungry."

"That makes sense, but can that be trusted?"

"Evidently all the people standing on line thought so!" They laughed.

"So you stand at the entrance to this giant cage and the trainer watches and reads the mood of the tiger. When he believes she's calm and ready, he calls you in—one person only— and tells you where to sit."

"Amazing! You actually sat with the tiger?"

"Yeah, I sat right next to her on her left about halfway down her side. I petted her a little. Her fur felt coarse, and her head moved around a little, and her tail swept back and forth. Then the trainer tells you when time is up, and you get up—very slowly—and go. Oh, and they take a picture of you when you're in there with the tiger as a souvenir!"

"Do you have it?"

"Yeah, but it's at home in a frame."

"That's awesome! I wish I could do that!" Sam pretended to be jealous.

As they continued walking, Sam still had his hands in his pockets. Silvia began feeling more relaxed with him so as they continued down a winding hill she put her hand around one of his arms.

Sam looked down and smiled. "That's better."

The two walked together like that until Silvia saw a big sign at a fork in the road. "Hey, up there is a petting zoo. You all want to go in?"

Even though Julie was afraid of dogs it was a unanimous vote, which surprised Silvia.

"I've never been inside the pen before," Julie admitted. "I get afraid sometimes. Are they friendly?"

"There are no dogs or dangerous animals in there, Julie, I promise." Silvia giggled. "Let's go this way." They walked up the hill to the petting zoo and found there was a short wait to go into the pen. While they waited, Zack guided them over to a tall vending machine that contained food for the animals.

"Here's a quarter. You put it in this machine, and when you turn the knob some food will come out. First, put your hand here." Zack inserted the coin for Julie then moved her hand into position and watched as the food pellets rolled down the chute. "Now, hold onto them until it's time to feed the llamas. When you're ready, you just put out your open hand and they'll lick the food right off of your palm."

"Really? I'm scared!" Julie jumped up and down.

"No, it'll be fun." Silvia tried to calm Julie's worries. "They don't bite or anything. I've done it a million times."

"Okay then, lead me to the llamas!"

They stood around the short fence that contained the llamas watching many children and their parents inside petting the animals. After a while, a group of people came out making room for others to go inside. Zack steered Julie toward a group of llamas while Silvia and Sam went to the left. Julie turned to watch Silvia feed the food pellets to the animals so she would know how to do it.

Without realizing Julie wasn't paying attention, Zack extended Julie's arm out in front of the mouths of the llamas, but her hand containing the pellets was still in a fist. Evidently, her closed hand was misinterpreted by one of the largest, most disagreeable llamas as being rude, so he spit a mucus-like substance all over her face and hair!

"A-a-a-h!" Julie screamed.

Zack was panic-stricken. "Oh my God! I'm so sorry!"

"Help me, Sil!" Julie screamed and ran out of the pen.

"Holy shit!" Silvia was shocked at the unfortunate sight. "Julie! Head to the ladies' room. It's right over there! I'm coming!"

As Silvia took off behind her, she couldn't help laughing at the gooey muck that covered her friend's head. Sam and Zack laughed as well but followed Silvia to the ladies' room to wait outside for the girls.

"Julie!" Silvia saw her friend standing at a sink in the corner. "Are you okay?" She couldn't stop the snorting sounds coming out of her nose.

"Why are you laughing?" Julie was leaning over the sink and scooping thick mucus out of her hair. "This is a disaster!"

"I'm sorry." Silvia strained to get control of herself by clearing her throat. "I know but . . . I'm sorry . . . I'm so sorry!"

"Look at me!" Julie screamed and gagged into the sink.

"Oh, honey!" Silvia watched the sticky substance leak all over the place and gagged a little herself. "I'm so sorry, Julie. Here let me help you."

Silvia grabbed some paper towels, ran them under the faucet, and began washing the milky goop off of Julie's head. In a few minutes, she was free of the disgusting substance but was soaked from the sopping wet paper towels.

"Now what do I do?" Julie cried a little more after seeing herself in the mirror. "I look like a drowned rat!"

Silvia grinned. "Come on, stop crying. You know I never go anywhere without my makeup and hairspray."

They dried Julie's face and hands with some napkins she had in her purse, and then Silvia positioned her head under the automatic hand dryer on the wall. It had a powerfully hot air stream, and with some brushing her hair dried quickly. Silvia then combed it into a stylish ponytail and fixed her face by applying a little foundation, mascara, and lipstick.

"See, much better."

"Thank you ... but I feel like such a fool!" Julie's eyes filled up again.

"Stop. You'll ruin your make-up." Silvia wiped away a lone tear. "Everything will be okay. I promise. Besides, it's important to keep a relationship interesting!" Julie giggled.

"And the good news is . . ." Silvia smiled back at Julie playfully and poked her on the nose. "I think Zack really likes you! I think you got a good one this time."

"Really? Okay. Do I look alright, Sil? Tell me the truth."

"Yes, honest, you look fine." Silvia admired her handy styling talents. "Now let's go out there. The guys are probably wondering if we slipped out the back and went home!"

"Really?"

"No, I'm kidding! Come on. You look great."

They exited the bathroom and saw Zack and Sam standing close by. As they approached the guys, Zack took his hands out from behind his back and presented Julie with a small bouquet of flowers.

"This is all I could find."

Silvia gasped and covered her mouth at Zack's thoughtful gesture.

Julie smiled with tears in her eyes and reached for the flowers. "Thank you. They're perfect."

Chapter 13

AS FALL CAME TO A close, the girls settled on a convenient date to meet for dinner. However, it was the same night they were scheduled to go to a wine tasting at a new Italian café bar called Mirabella. They weren't set to leave until eight o'clock, so Liza prepared chicken cacciatore and potatoes to make sure they all had a substantial meal.

Silvia arrived last and, after her usual welcome by Little Bucket, she followed the incredible aroma into the sunroom where the girls were just beginning to eat. Of course, Liza was dressed to the nines in a lovely black suit with a ruffled blouse and long white pearls. The rest of the girls were also wearing black (the signature color for a New York evening event), however their outfits were more in tune with a relaxed, low-key affair.

"Yum. I can't wait!" Silvia finished sipping her water then hurried to make her plate and sit down.

Liza picked up her phone. "Hey, I meant to send this to you girls. I received a video of my show from the director at the elder facility. Let's all watch it."

Before anyone could speak, Liza pressed a button on her phone and held it so everyone could watch—the girls couldn't believe they had to sit through it again! At the end, she acknowledged there might have been a few inappropriate choices in her material, but she still insisted she wasn't all that bad.

"I say, 'yeah me!' Granted, some of what I said could have been more . . . well, delicate, I suppose. But all in all, I thought it was pretty good for my second time . . . And I looked fabulous, right?" Liza stared at her friends.

Maybe she wants our opinions after all, thought Silvia.

"Yes, you looked like a real performer. That's for sure!" Julie smiled and nodded.

"I love the pin-up girls joke!" Liza giggled. "Angela Lansbury . . . hilarious!"

"Yes, that joke did 'murder' them!" Sarah quipped, referencing the star's television series, *Murder She Wrote*.

"B-o-o-o! That's a bad joke. Liza, don't use that!" Julie chuckled.

Tina smiled. "I think the bingo bit was my favorite. I love picturing sweet little old ladies cussing at one another!"

"Now there's a surprise." Silvia giggled then turned her attention back to Liza. "So, tell me, what do you think could have been improved upon?"

"Well, I don't know," she sighed. "I'm trying to tell jokes that relate to the audience I'm speaking to. This is hard, ya know."

"Yes, you're right, it is but . . . and I'm just suggesting this . . . As you choose material that relates to the crowd you're entertaining, you might want to eliminate some of the jokes that . . . well, insult them." Silvia cringed hoping she didn't hurt Liza's feelings.

Liza tilted her head. "What do you mean?"

"Silvia's right." Julie nodded. "Teasing is one thing, but you have to make your audience laugh at themselves . . . not feel badly about their lives. Can you see the difference, Liza?"

"H-m-m-m." They could almost hear the pistons in Liza's mind bobbing up and down.

"Why don't you try some self-deprecating humor? You know, make fun of some things about yourself too—like the pros do." Silvia took another mouthful of food.

"What? Give me an example."

"Okay." Silvia thought for a moment while chewing. "What about Rodney Dangerfield? Wait, let me google him on my phone."

"That's a good idea, Sil." Tina nodded. "He's the master at that."

Silvia soon found the site. "Here's one. Rodney Dangerfield said, 'My psychiatrist told me I was crazy, so I told him I wanted another opinion. He said fine, you're ugly too.' See what I mean?" Liza giggled.

Sarah nodded. "And my aunt always tells the same joke about going to the movies when she's with my relatives. She says, 'Just remember, it's better to pay full price than to admit you're a senior citizen.' See? She's making fun of her age, of being old, and she believes it makes the kids laugh. Well, it used to, but after so many times—"

"Here's another one!" Julie also found some Dangerfield jokes. "He said, 'This morning when I put on my underwear, I could hear the Fruit of the Loom guys laughing at me.'" The girls chuckled. "Get it now, Liza?"

Tina finished eating. "Wait. You know, Joan Rivers also did that type of comedy."

"Oh, right! Let me find one of her jokes." Silvia tapped on her phone. "Here's one: 'I have no sex appeal. The only time I hear heavy breathing from my husband's side of the bed is when he's having an asthma attack.'"

Tina laughed. "I love it!"

"Here's another," Silvia continued. "'My vagina is like Newark. Men know it's there, but they don't want to visit.'"

Julie giggled into her hand. "Oh my God! She kills me! Understand, Liza?"

"Yeah, I think so. Thanks, girls. I appreciate it."

"Hey, has anyone seen the invitation for this wine tasting?" Tina began looking around and found it on the refrigerator. She opened the invitation and the brochure. "This place looks gorgeous! How did you get an invite anyway, Liza?"

"Thomas." She was chewing on some red hot candies.

"Oh my God!" Silvia tried to take Liza's candy away. "You're gonna get sick!"

Sarah laughed while the two wrestled. "They have some kind of red hot liqueur now, you know."

"Really?"

"Great."

Tina continued reading through the brochure. "Here's a list of some of the wines and their descriptions, which we may or may not be tasting."

"Read some." Silvia put her plate down on the table and rubbed her belly. "I was starving . . . I ate too fast!"

Tina was used to pronouncing French words, so the words rolled off her tongue. "Okay, it says there's . . . Duckhorn Sauvignon Blanc, a combination of ripe citrus, melon, and white flowers; a Trimbach Riesling that tastes like lemon peel, florals, and fruit flavors; and Hudelot-Noellat Bourgogne, an entry-level burgundy."

"I don't know anything about wine," admitted Julie.

Sara nodded. "Me neither. I just taste it, and if I like it, I drink it."

"Let me try." Silvia laughed and took the brochure from Tina. She looked through the list and began to mumble. "Forget it, I give up!"

Soon it was time for the group to head out to the wine tasting. They didn't know this would be the last event they would attend together for a while.

As the weeks passed, Liza got the job as a file clerk at the company Thomas recommended. She also continued to work diligently on her stand-up comedy, utilizing the advice given by her friends and practicing on people affiliated with some other small charity organizations throughout the city. She was anxious to surprise her girlfriends with new, better-quality material.

Tina was working non-stop because Niki was spending a lot of time out of the country with her family. She told Tina that her husband wasn't feeling well after their trip to the Caribbean, so they headed directly back to France. The fact that she was put in charge invigorated her, and the priceless on-the-job training proved to be the best thing that could have happened to her. She managed the daily operations effortlessly and proved to Niki she could handle even the money end of the business successfully.

Sarah became even more depressed; just going through the motions at work and dreading every moment. Mary Louise's interference had gotten worse. That woman grilled her on every document submission and questioned her every decision. Sarah sent out her résumé to other departments and various companies and was functioning solely on the belief that one of the places she queried would respond to her with an interview request soon.

Julie was now spending most of her time with Zack. After that humiliating date at the zoo, they became inseparable. Who knew getting llama snot blown all over your head would get you a boyfriend! Every time she spoke with her friends, all she talked about was Zack. Her enthusiasm and praise led the girls to believe she had fallen hard for him, and they prayed she wouldn't get hurt again. There were reports of meeting relatives, spending a weekend away, and even talk of moving in together.

Silvia was still proofreading at work, but also began spending some time with her new semi-boyfriend, Sam Newell—the shy guy from the zoo date. They weren't all that serious yet, but they were having fun together and she was trying hard to follow Julie's example to keep an open heart. Unfortunately, she also became a bit depressed about her job and wondered if her writing would ever get published. She began having anxiety and panic attacks several times a week due to some buried memories from her childhood resurfacing, so she decided to seek professional help.

At a friend's recommendation, Silvia began seeing Dr. Wesley Yosef. Dr. Yosef was a wonderful therapist who specialized in adult cognitive therapy and was rated five stars on Yelp. He was an older man with big, kind brown eyes who always wore a suit and tie and had a meticulously groomed mustache and beard. He was easy to talk to, very interactive, and immediately helped put her at ease. She grew to trust him and slowly opened up about her heartbreaking past. In her sessions she shared some memories that highlighted how she was denied any attention, love, or guidance which culminated in her depression, and her self-esteem and trust issues.

Silvia was the only child of two self-absorbed, disengaged parents, Edith and Roberto Cruz. Her mother was a beautiful, light mix of Italian, Greek, and Irish, and her father was mostly Cuban with olive skin and a head full of dark hair. Even from a very young age there was little attention or involvement in her life by her parents. She was forced to confront the obstacles and suffer the humiliations of growing up basically all alone.

The family was somewhat poor, but not destitute. The little money they had coming in was earned by her working mother and quickly gambled away by her out-of-work father. Though he always claimed to be "trying" to work, her father's talent was creating and filing disability claims. The insurance checks he received subsidized his habit of spending most of their money at the dog track. His time at home each day was brief, just long enough for Silvia to get home from school in the afternoon and for her mother to return from work in the evening. When he was at home he was busy making notations in the margins of his track book and smoking cigarettes while rebuffing his daughter's attempts to connect with him. He truly believed his persistence and focused attention would enable him to mathematically calculate the winning dog in each race. He was convinced the big payoff was just around the corner. It never came.

Though he never sought out or even welcomed his daughter's company, that didn't stop Silvia from trying. A recurrent request from her was about building the fort in the backyard that he kept promising. The first twenty times she asked she would bound excitedly into the room and ask him about it, to which he would reply, "I can't right now. I'm busy. Tomorrow." After a while, however, she dreaded hearing his response and instead would slowly creep into the room, sweating and shaking and hoping that this time he might say "Yes." She truly believed that one day it would happen, and every time he told her "Tomorrow," she believed him.

One day her mother overheard her begging her father to build the fort and, for whatever reason, confronted Silvia and told her to wake up! She told her daughter plainly that her father was lying and that he was never, ever going to build any fort for her. Silvia was stunned by her mother's careless and shocking announcement. It felt like a slap in the face from both of them. She was hurt and embarrassed and felt as though the bottom had fallen out of her world. She was traumatized—both mentally and physically. But her father promised! Why would he lie? How could she be so stupid? She quickly realized she would never know the answers to her questions and pushed down her pain and confusion. As for her parents, it worked out well—her mother was relieved of her whining, and her father finally got to be left alone.

Silvia was also never taught the social skills most people acquire in their youth, so school for her was a long and confusing nightmare. She had no idea how to interact with other children. Her idea of making friends with another child was to give them her belongings—costume jewelry, a toy, a record album—anything she had to make them like her. She was bullied a lot by the girls in school, too, even though all the boys in her class liked her and always tried to kiss her. That might have been one reason the other girls hated her. Unfortunately, she also dressed differently than the other girls, usually wearing her cousins' hand-me-downs which were too big and out of style.

Another thing Silvia believed were her father's habitual "exaggerations" and his in-and-out existence in a make-believe world where he invented things and was consulted by important people to do important tasks. Upon hearing her father discussing such things with other adults, she would go to school and naïvely repeat these irrational delusions to the other kids who would, in turn, go home and repeat them to their parents. At school the following day, there would be taunting and threatening the gullible, bragging child. As a result, Silvia went to school each morning feeling nervous, frightened, and unable to take a deep breath until she returned home in the afternoon.

It was no surprise Silvia quickly realized she was happier being alone. It took an enormous amount of energy to stay alert and carefully monitor what she said and did, and she found it nearly impossible to detect the true intentions of others. She grew to believe people were mean and wanted to destroy her. She found safety and comfort in the peace and quiet of her bedroom—no enemies approaching, no humiliating surprises, and nothing to worry about except what her mind conjured.

Silvia wondered at an early age why her life was this way. The other kids had mothers who stayed home, made cookies, and played with them, while their fathers worked all week and took them to ball games on the weekend. She was convinced that she was the child who had been purposely picked out by God to be that one, odd kid every neighborhood had. The one who looked different; the one whose family was peculiar; the one who walked by the moms who would mumble, "That girl is odd," or "There's something wrong with that child," or "Kids, don't you play with her." The comments and sideways looks would crush her, but somehow she managed to struggle through each day maneuvering through the minefields of ignorance and sporting the armor that would deflect the missiles of degradation hurled at her by the world.

The one thing Silvia had in her favor was, although she wasn't people smart, she was book smart. She studied and did her homework eagerly and pretty much aced all her tests. The teachers loved her, and she loved them. Being a teacher's pet gave the other kids yet another reason to bully her. Her parents were proud of her excellent report cards and the teachers' positive comments on her papers. For those she got pats on the head and a few words of recognition, which satisfied their parental responsibilities and confirmed their assumptions their child was fine. They never noticed their daughter's inappropriate behavior patterns, ill-attempts at developing relationships, and low self-image, which were in the process of forming an unhappy, dysfunctional adult. They were blind to the anxiety their daughter felt each moment of every day, trying not to draw attention to herself, to fit in with the other kids, to survive.

Silvia explained to Dr. Yosef that even haircuts given to her by her mother exacerbated her ordeal. In the kitchen with a towel wrapped around her neck, her mother would cut her bangs by eyeing the line of wavy hair resting on her forehead. She knew all too well that mom-butchered haircuts were fodder for harassment by the other kids, not to mention humiliating school pictures.

Time after time she begged her mother for a professional haircut which would allow her to fit in with her classmates. Finally, her mother gave in. That day, she walked down to the local "beauty parlor" and told the heavily sprayed, high-haired hairdresser she wanted her hair cut into a layered style, which she hoped would make her look more normal. After reviewing her new look in the cloudy mirror, she skipped home feeling like a movie star—that is, until she examined her hair more closely in the mirror after the wind and humidity had settled in. She realized that although she said "layered," the stylist heard "mullet." The only thing worse than the long thin curtain of hair at her neck was her natural curly hair rebelling against the shorter cuts made to the top. Regrettably, she ended up looking more like a rabid poodle than a pretty schoolgirl.

While this experience could be viewed as a small bump in the road for another child, for Silvia it was disastrous. Though she pleaded for help through a barrage of tears, her mother's attitude was indifferent and her efforts were minimal. Her solution was spraying on a little Aqua Net and telling her daughter to stop being so dramatic. It was unclear to her whether her mother was uncaring or disinclined to believe the severity of her anguish. However, on Monday her fears were confirmed as her new look sparked merciless name-calling and threats of violence toward the defenseless child. Recess that day ended as most of the others had—with Silvia cowering in a corner as the crowd of children berated her until the school bell rang.

Aside from her situation at school, Silvia explained to Dr. Yosef that she felt like an outcast even on the rare occasion when her family was all together. Once a year they would take a vacation—or what her parents perceived to be a vacation. Because they didn't have much money, their choices were limited but not impossible. The opportunities for people such as these were few; however, the obvious option was to go visit and mooch off of relatives.

One week in July, Silvia and her parents would climb into the Buick and drive to Aunt Junie's house on Cape Cod in Massachusetts—a trip Silvia dreaded every year. It was an agonizing five to six hour drive with no radio ("You'll drain the battery," her father said), and no open windows ("I don't want to mess my hair," said her mother), while she lay in the back seat under her blanket and pillow trying not to breathe in the thickly-settled cigarette smoke disseminated by both parents.

On the way, they would stop only once or twice to quickly use the restrooms and grab a snack, and then it was back into the Cheech and Chong mobile. When they reached the Bourne Bridge (which connects Cape Cod to the rest of Massachusetts), she knew it wasn't much farther to Aunt Junie's house and would beg for the windows to be opened. Thanks to cooler temperatures and traffic on the Cape, her parents would agree and finally roll down the windows. Within seconds, Silvia would stick her whole head out of the Buick like a greyhound chasing a rabbit at the dog track—eyes wide and mouth open gulping in fresh air!

Once they arrived at Aunt Junie's house, her parents would slowly get out of the car and stretch their bodies as Silvia, gray with nausea, crawled out from the back seat onto the ground. Soon relatives and neighbors would come out to greet her parents with smiles and hugs while looking disappointedly down at the annoying, sullen child moaning and rolling around on the grass. After the crowd moved into the house, the inevitable spewing of watery vomit would follow, enabling her to stand again and make her way into the house dragging her now stinky pillow, blanket, and suitcase behind her.

There were few children her age there so, although she was bored, at least she had a break from her time back home (she spent summers mostly alone in her room). She would sit and watch the adults tell stories, debate political issues, and talk about losing weight while stuffing their faces with homemade goodies brought over by the neighbors. The men would eat deli sandwiches and fruit (mostly watermelon and oranges) for lunch, then stroll around the neighborhood criticizing all the lawns and foundations. In the afternoon, they would sit and listen to her father brag about his big ideas while her mother sat with the women and rolled her eyes. In the evenings, they would entertain the neighbors by sharing stories of themselves in their younger, happier days. On at least one night during the vacation, they would drink wine and reminisce while watching old reel-to-reel home movies projected onto a white stone wall in the backyard. At the end of the week, it was the return to a slow death in the badass Buick to make the agonizing road trip all over again.

When asked specifically about spending time with just her father, Silvia could only remember one such memory—the one Saturday her father invited her to do some errands with him.

She was so excited when he reached out to her and even dared to feel wanted. At that time, her father drove a black Pontiac Grand Prix, which made her feel like she was riding in the Batmobile. They jumped in the car and hit the road stopping first at the Savings & Loan. Her father got out and told her to stay put so he could double park in front of the bank. She was excited when he returned and looked forward to another stop. Next, they went to the dentist office. Once again, her father told her to stay in the car, promising he would be back quickly. As her father took longer and longer to return, she slowly became hysterical, fearing he had abandoned her. Forty-five minutes later, he returned to find her whimpering with hurt feelings and a stomachache in the front seat. Their third and final stop was the bakery. This time he said nothing; he left the car running and his daughter devastated as he ran in and bought a pie for his wife.

As for her time alone with her mother, Silvia recalled one occasion when her mother invited her to go to the movies. After one of her aunts suggested she spend more time with her daughter, her mother made the offer and planned the day.

On that special day, they took a taxicab downtown to a movie theater showing a rather racy R-rated movie. Sure, screw Disney. Though Silvia was a bit confused, she didn't care because she was spending an afternoon with her mother. At the end of the movie as the credits rolled, her mother turned to her in the dimly lit theater and asked, "Do you want to see another movie?" More time with mom—a dream come true! As they began to walk out of the movie theater, her mother stopped her at the exit.

Silvia waited, and after a few minutes her mother peeked her head out to see if anyone was there. She then grabbed Silvia's hand and rushed her down the red carpeted hall to the entrance of another movie. When Silvia realized they didn't have tickets to the second movie, she stopped dead in her tracks.

"What are you doing?"

"Lower your voice," her mother whispered cheerfully. "We're going to sneak into the movie. Won't that be fun?"

"No!" Silvia dropped to the floor in protest, knowing this was wrong.

Afraid of drawing attention, her mother tried to drag her daughter's limp body into the theater. She was not expecting her daughter's reaction. Silvia continued to rebuff her mother's efforts and screamed so loudly that several young movie theater ushers appeared on the scene to investigate. Standing there was a tall, skinny boy with a face full of acne and the swagger of John Wayne.

Her mother became infuriated at having to explain herself to mere children. While concealing what she had planned to do, she pleaded with her daughter to get up but to no avail. Eventually, she sighed angrily and announced they were going home.

With her mother enraged and embarrassed, they left the theater, hailed a taxi, and rode silently all the way home. As they climbed the stairs to their apartment, her mother continued to ignore the poor child who was aghast and devastated by the day's turnabout. At the top landing, her mother looked disparagingly at Silvia. "You ruin everything," she said, then turned and slammed the door. With those heart-breaking words, the destroyed child headed back to her room—the only place in the world that made any sense.

Silvia explained to Dr. Yosef that for most of her childhood she tried her best to decipher the abundance of mixed messages she received from her parents. Her encounters with them made her feel like she was on a rollercoaster of emotion often leaving her damaged and disoriented. However, there was a small part of her that refused to believe that their reckless interactions with her were intentional. She wondered if they were just lashing out as a result of their own unhappy lives or if they were even cognizant of the impact of their cold words and actions. This observation by Silvia at such a young age gave Dr. Yosef some insight into the intelligence and survival skills of his patient.

Dr. Yosef also asked Silvia to talk about the passing of her mother. Silvia described how when she turned eighteen, her mother suffered a horribly drawn-out death from ovarian cancer. Right after she passed away, her father went off on his own and never again contacted her. She was once more left alone to find a way to make a living and pick up the pieces of her pitiful, now adult life.

With her father gone, she was forced to vacate the apartment she had shared with her parents. The only call she received before leaving was from her Aunt Junie. However, she did not call to help Silvia; she called to complain about her family and to dredge up sad, old memories. After listening to her aunt go on and on, she became filled with anxiety and started to physically shake. Finally reaching her limit, Silvia broke down herself. The truth spewed from her mouth like a volcano, dumbfounding her aunt and silencing her cruel, judgmental words. Before hanging up, however, her aunt felt the need to repeat the same words she heard often over the years when the so-called adults had nothing else to offer. "Life is what we make it, always has been, always will be." *Thank you, Aunt Junie. That ought to help me put food on my table.*

From everything she told him, Dr. Yosef surmised that Silvia's keen mind, will to live, and sense of humor had, and would continue to, aid her in healing from her past and living a fruitful life. The doctor came to believe it was a miracle Silvia Cruz was able to function so successfully and could lead a relatively normal life after a childhood filled with so much neglect, depression, and fear.

Chapter 14

IT WAS DISCUSSED IN ONE therapy session that it would be healthy for Silvia to interact more with the world and explore different interests. Dr. Yosef said it might help her put her past to rest if she pursued her "joy" and welcomed new activities and people into her life. He pointed out how closed off she had become, so she promised him that she would give it a try. As she contemplated what might make her happy, she was surprised one Saturday by an opportunity conveyed to her by her hairdresser, Vicki.

"Hi. Did I forget something?"

"No. Right after you left, my next client sat down and asked about you. He saw you walking out and is very interested in you."

"Really? Who is he?"

"He's an attorney," said Vicki, "very successful. He has money, never been married, and owns his own home . . . a good catch, I would say."

"I don't know. What does he look like?" She had to ask even though she felt very superficial.

"He has full, dark hair. I style it for him every couple of weeks. Not a Greek god, mind you, but nice looking, and he wants your phone number."

"No!" Her stomach dropped. *Interact more with the world . . . Welcome new people . . . Damn!*

"Um . . . If he wants to meet, set it up for Wednesday night. I can meet him for drinks. Then text me the when and where."

When Sylvia hung up, she couldn't believe what she had done. This had disaster written all over it. *I'm doomed*, she thought. *Uh-oh. I shouldn't have said that. Maybe I should spit three times.*

Wednesday came and, of course, Silvia was regretting her decision to meet this mysterious lawyer. It was the day of the date, so it would be rude to cancel last minute. After work, she freshened up her make-up in the ladies' room, but didn't change clothes. She sprayed on a little perfume, straightened out her long, eggplant-colored blazer and loose trousers, and headed to the specified meeting place—a pub-style restaurant called The End Zone.

She arrived promptly at eight and walked into the bar looking for a man meeting the description given to her by Vicki. She didn't spot anyone whom she thought fit the bill, so she decided to sit at the bar to see if her date might find her. Soon she was approached by a short, pale, thin man with bushy black hair wearing a V-neck sweater and a gold chain. She suddenly wished Little Bucket was nearby.

"Silvia?"

"Ken?" *Please God, don't let this be him.*

"Hi. How are you?" he asked. "Thanks for coming." He was smiling from ear to ear.

As Silvia stood up to follow Ken to the table he had been holding, she realized she was taller than he was. He did have a thick head of hair, but it turned out to be a hairpiece.

This is karma getting me back for laughing at Uncle Morty's memorial, right? Thanks a lot.

As she sat down across from him she thought he looked familiar. The waitress came over immediately (*God bless her!*), and they ordered drinks.

"I'll have another scotch." He smiled and winked at her.

Silvia needed something strong. "I'll have a vodka martini, please."

"So, were you surprised by the call from Vicki?"

"Yeah, I was." She wondered again why he looked so familiar.

"I have to admit when I saw you, I was instantly attracted. You have such beautiful hair." He reached his hand across to touch it.

"Oh, thank you. Vicki's been taking care of this mess for a long time." She shook her hair around so he would stop.

"Me too. I'll only let her style mine too."

Style your wig, you mean.

Soon the waitress came back with their drinks and asked if they wanted to order some food. The two perused the bar menu, discussed their choices, and finally agreed on splitting two appetizers. By then she was ready for another martini.

Though it was dimly lit in the restaurant, sitting here on the bar side with the lights from the many televisions on the walls made it a bit brighter. They praised the talents of their matchmaking hairdresser, and Ken raised a glass to her. While he took a sip from his scotch, she zeroed in on his hair again. *I gotta stop staring at that thing.*

Ken began talking about his successful law practice and his local political contacts. Silvia was relieved he was chatty because she was at a loss for words. He also told her where he liked to go on vacation and all about his new, beautiful, state-of-the-art home.

"My house is still pretty much empty and it could sure use a woman's touch."

He's trying to seduce me with all his money to get me over there!

"Oh, really. I'm no decorator."

"Well, I can certainly see you have style, Silvia." He slowly reached for her hand across the table. "It would mean a lot to me if you would come over and take a look."

Just then the waitress returned with her second martini. "Just a few more minutes on the appetizers."

She pulled her hand away and reached for her fresh, life-saving cocktail. "So, what kind of cases do you handle?"

As predicted, he rambled on about the personal injury cases he won and the strategizing involved in order to beat the insurance companies. He then described in detail some of the horrific wounds and amputations suffered by his clients. *Gross!*

Soon the martinis began kicking in, and Silvia started to relax. Her attention wandered and she began looking at the televisions on the walls around the bar while still hearing "blah, blah, blah" from Atticus Finch across the table. As she focused momentarily on the wall behind Ken's head, her eyes flew open wide.

There he was! That's how she knew him. He was that Ken Gold! The lawyer who did all those awful commercials for his personal injury law firm was her date! "Go with Gold. Your case is worth it!" was his slogan. *Ew! This can't be happening.*

Her eyes began darting from the television to Ken and back many times, as if doing so would make it not be true. When he finally took a breath from bragging about settlement amounts, he turned around to see what was holding Silvia's attention.

"Oh, yeah. That's me." He laughed and waited for a reaction.

"Yes, it is." She gulped down the rest of her martini. "I thought I recognized you."

"Let me tell you, those babies bring in lots of business. People know I can get them the most money for their cases, and my record's practically unmatched."

When he finally stopped boasting, he smiled exactly the way he did in the commercials and she threw up a little in her mouth.

"Really," she mumbled through her napkin while waiving wildly for the waitress. "That's terrific." *Terrific? I never say "terrific." What was happening?!*

The waitress finally came over with their food and she ordered another martini. Ken reached over to distribute even portions of food onto their plates as she sipped from her fresh drink.

"I may have to drive you home, young lady." He had observed the amount and speed with which she was consuming alcohol.

Oh shit, she thought, *I can't get drunk. No way is this guy driving me home.*

Silvia grabbed her glass of water and took a few gulps. "No, this is my limit, and once I eat, I'll be fine."

While they were picking at the appetizers, a couple of people stopped by the table to say hello and shake Ken's hand.

They must be congratulating him on finally being accompanied by a woman.

"Wow, fans?"

He laughed. "No, I come here a lot. They all know me here." All of a sudden, the crowd cheered at something that was happening on the giant television in the back of the room.

"Great, we're winning!" He became fixated on the game.

Silvia turned to the television for a few moments as well, grateful for a break from his constant staring and a chance to wolf down some food to soak up the alcohol. Soon, another man stopped by and began what sounded like a business conversation with Ken.

As the man turned to leave, she panicked. "Hey, why don't you sit down and finish your conversation?"

"You sure?" the man asked.

"Sure." She drank some more water. "No worries."

"You got a nice lady here," the man said.

"I know." Ken smiled proudly.

Ick!

She was now having a panic attack. She wasn't one to hurt anyone's feelings but being here with this odd little man was excruciating. She should have never agreed to a blind date.

I've got to get the hell out of here!

While the men were talking, she excused herself to the ladies' room where she took some deep breaths and began to fix her face. As she looked in the mirror, she laughed out loud at her karmic predicament, then threw her lipstick back in her bag without applying.

You got me, Uncle Morty!

She headed back to the table and about halfway there she noticed the other man was gone.

"Hi!" Ken was smiling ear to ear and waving.

Once back at the table, Silvia began her exit speech. "Look, I'm sorry, but I'm really not feeling well, Ken. I think it was a mix of the drinks and fried food. I need to get going."

He looked disappointed. "Oh really? Okay well, let me drive you home."

"No, no, no, that's okay. I'll just end up getting car sick. I'm already feeling nauseated. If you don't mind, I'm just going to see myself home. The night air will do me good." She grabbed her things and turned to leave. "Thank you. It was nice meeting you."

Ken took a sip of his scotch. "Are you still coming over to take a look at my house?" When he turned around for the answer, Silvia was already out of sight.

Chapter 15

IT WAS A COLD DECEMBER night when the girls met up again at Liza's for dinner. They were all looking forward to a fun meal of burgers and hotdogs with corn on the cob and fries while catching up on the many changes in each of their lives. When Silvia arrived, she retched into Little Bucket then walked out of the bathroom to see her friends sitting in the sunroom—everyone except Julie.

"Come on! I thought everyone was coming. Where's Julie?" Silvia slumped on the couch.

"She just called." Liza was sitting in the giant shoe uncharacteristically wearing a long, loose t-shirt and comfortable elastic waist pants. "She'll be here any minute. She wanted to make sure we were all here."

As soon as Silvia grabbed a cold bottle of water, they heard loud footsteps bounding up the stairs.

"Sounds like you, Sil."

"I know."

Within seconds, bouncing through the door came Julie. Without even saying hello, she held up her left hand and screamed, "I'm engaged!"

The girls all jumped up from their squatted positions, attacked her with kisses and hugs, and took turns admiring her ring.

Julie was beaming. "Can you believe it? I'm so happy!"

"That's fucking beautiful!" Tina studied the stone closely with the expert eye of a jeweler. "So brilliant and two and a half carats! I'm jealous!"

"O-o-o-h, a rare compliment from Tina!" Silvia admired the ring. "That means it's a fine diamond because Tina knows her stuff."

They all surrounded Julie until finally she had enough. "Okay, quit shaking me. I'm not a martini!"

She took off her coat and grabbed a plate. Still gushing about the news, everyone rushed to get their food, excited to hear her tell her engagement story.

"So tell us. How did he do it?" Liza tapped Julie's leg.

Tina stared at her hand again. "And where did he get that ring?"

"It's a family heirloom." Julie gazed lovingly at her hand. "It was really very sweet. We were driving through the city yesterday, and we came to the zoo. I jokingly screamed something about having PTSD from the llama attack." Everyone giggled.

"Right then he took a left into the zoo and started laughing. So I figured he was busting my onions. He said, 'That's it, we're going in to see the llamas—you have to face your fears!' He parked the car and told me to get out. It was freezing and I was kind of freaking out thinking he was really going to drag me in there to the llamas, but I gave in . . . curious to see how far he was going with this joke and . . ." she began to tear up.

"As we started walking up to the entrance, I realized he wasn't beside me. So I turned around, and there he was on one knee holding the ring out. I ran back to him, and he said, 'I knew I loved you since the moment I saw llama boogers on your head, and my love for you has grown every day since. Julie, will you marry me?'"

"Oh my God, I got the chicken skin!" Liza rubbed her arm. "I love that story even though it has the word 'boogers' in it!"

"And the zoo is closed, Julie. So he knew at some point you'd have to turn back around. A brilliant plan!" Silvia sighed and leaned back.

Julie laughed, "Oh yeah!"

"And you're roommates now too. How's that going?" Sarah giggled.

Julie blushed. "Good, it's weird though. He's so nice! I keep waiting for him to scream, 'Why isn't my dinner on the table?!'" The girls chuckled. "And did I tell you I pet some dogs in the park? It was so fun. Now I can't believe I was ever afraid of them!"

"Good for you!" Liza clapped. "Are you going to get one?"

"No, but we took in two cats from Zack's friend who was moving. They're named Chloe and Windy . . . because Windy farts constantly."

"That's great. Good practice for babies later." Liza winked and smiled.

"Uh-huh!" Julie shook her head. "So I hear you've been practicing some new routines?"

"Yes! I've been working very hard too. Girls, I can't wait for you to see me! I think I finally found my modi operandus!"

"Modus operandi." Silvia smiled as the girls sat there looking puzzled. "She means she found her groove. Her . . . comedic formula! We're so happy for you Liza!"

Then Tina smiled and tapped Sarah. "Go ahead. Tell them your news."

Sarah beamed. "I got a new job! I started this past Monday at the Department of Banking and Insurance!"

"No more Mary Louise!" Everyone cheered.

Tina nodded. "Yes! And you're already looking much happier. You look really good!"

"I love my new job—thanks to my new friend, Joanna. It's challenging and the people are great, and I get to walk Whiskey Sour every day on my lunch hour without being scolded like a child. It's awesome!" Sarah and Tina high-fived each other.

"How's the spa, Tina? You had some construction done, right?"

"Yes, and the updates are just about done. It's gorgeous. I sent pictures to Niki in France, and she loves it! I'm so fucking proud of myself!" She jokingly patted herself on the shoulder. "You should all come in one day for a complimentary sauna and massage!"

"We're there!" Liza bounced in her chair.

The conversation came full circle to Julie again as the girls asked her questions about the kind of wedding she wanted. She said she had not even started to think about it, so they found themselves reminiscing about old boyfriends and the creepy guys they met over the years.

Liza put her plate down on the table after having a second corn on the cob. "I gotta remember I ate those when I go to the bathroom later!" Tina and Julie moaned.

"Anyway, I remember one summer when I was in my twenties ..." Liza wiped her mouth. "I met this guy at a club in the city. He was dressed in a suit and tie. He told me he was a very successful car salesman and asked me for a date. So, one night we went to a movie and took a walk. He was a perfect gentleman—no kissing, no touching. At the time I was staying with a friend in an elevator building, so when he drove me home I said goodnight, gave him a quick peck, and got out of the car. He also got out, insisting on seeing me to my door. What a gentleman, I thought." She stood up to act out the rest of the story.

"So in the elevator I pushed the button to my floor, and when I turned back around, his pants were down around his ankles! He was standing there with this gargantuan pecker hanging out! I mean, it was . . . Oh my God!" All the girls screamed with laughter.

"Now, I just stood there. I couldn't speak. He looked at me and said, 'I just wanted you to see what I got.'" The girls screamed.

"I couldn't help it, but I stared at the huge thing—probably longer than I should have, and then I looked up at him." Liza laughed even louder and paused to catch her breath. "I was stunned and a little scared too, ya know . . . hoping he wasn't going to attack me because he just whipped it out! Once the elevator stopped at my floor, I jumped out, and right before the doors closed, he pulled his pants back up and said, 'Thanks, I had fun!'"

The girls continued laughing as Julie leaned over closer to Liza. "How big was it?"

"I never saw anything . . . I bet it was as big as that porn guy who got famous for his giant schlong. What's his name?"

"John Holmes," said Sarah with a straight face, elevating the laughter to another level. Everyone stared at her in shock that the porn star's name rolled quickly and effortlessly off her tongue.

Tina got up to get another drink and tilted her head toward Sarah. "I guess you can't judge a book by its cover, huh?" Sarah nodded, but didn't understand the comment was directed at her.

Silvia covered her giggles and whispered to Liza, "So did you ever see him again?"

"Every time I closed my eyes for a whole year!"

Julie sighed and shook her head. "Why are men such idiots?"

Tina shrugged. "To give us funny stories to tell when we're old."

"See Julie, you aren't the only one who ever met a loser!" Silvia giggled.

All of a sudden, Liza burst into tears, which caught everyone by surprise.

Sarah immediately turned around. "What's the matter?"

Tina shrugged her shoulders. "Maybe she misses him."

Silvia got a bad feeling. "What's wrong, Liza?"

"I'm sorry, girls." Liza was sobbing.

Julie jumped up. "But we were just laughing, and you told that funny story. What happened?"

Liza tried to smile as tears rolled down her cheeks. "I know. I'm just a mess right now. I'm sorry." The girls formed a supportive circle around her and waited for her to calm down before pressing for more details.

"I don't want to ruin our night, but I have to tell you all something. I've been waiting until we were all together. I'm sorry, Julie. I had no idea you were going to come here with such wonderful news."

Julie nodded compassionately. "That's okay. What's the matter?"

Silvia held Liza's hand while she continued crying for another few minutes. She finally wiped her eyes and moved to the edge of her chair to be closer to the group. "I just found out . . ." she said slowly, "I got the cancer."

The girls sat there flabbergasted. Silvia felt sick to her stomach. Liza had just spoken the words every woman silently prayed she would never have to say. Now, as her friends cried with her, she passed around her box of tissues.

"What kind? Where is it?" Silvia whispered.

"It's breast cancer." Liza was beginning to get control of herself. "The good news is, Dr. Melvin told me it's a very, very small cell in my left breast. Luckily, it was found right away in my last mammogram."

No one took their eyes off Liza as she spoke so bravely about her diagnosis.

"Of course, they know that because I had a biopsy, and they tested the sample and looked at the scans. The doctors I saw all agreed we gotta remove the little fucker as soon as possible so it doesn't spread. Then depending on the patheology, I may or may not need radiation or chemotherapy."

"You mean 'pathology.'" Silvia wiped her face and smiled gently. "It's gonna be okay. We can deal with this. It's small, caught early, and you have a good plan of action."

"When are you having the surgery?" Julie was still tearing up.

"In a couple of weeks. I'm going in for . . ." She paused, took a deep breath, and continued, "a double mastectomy."

"Both?" Sarah was shocked. Most of the girls were stunned by this swift and radical decision and worried about what Liza was about to go through.

"Yes. They said it's best to take them both even when you see cancer in just one."

"Good!" Silvia patted Liza on the leg. "I truly believe that's the right decision. I saw Dr. Melvin last year for a shadow they saw on my mammogram. Thank God, it turned out to be nothing, but that's exactly what I would have done."

Liza was surprised and a bit relieved. "So you know Dr. Melvin? You think he's good?"

"Yes, he's excellent, and you're right. They say, depending on the kind of cancer you have, once a woman has cancer in one breast, there's like an eighty-five percent chance it will spread to the other. You've got to be quick and aggressive and take them both so you don't have to go through it a second time . . . especially if cancer runs in your family." Silvia watched Liza begin to feel a bit more optimistic.

"Yeah, that's what Dr. Melvin said."

Julie opened her eyes wide. "And that's what Angelina Jolie did."

"That's right." Sarah nodded in agreement. "So why didn't you tell us about your mammogram, Sil?"

"I was just so grateful it was nothing, and I didn't really want to talk about it. But Dr. Melvin is the best around." Silvia reassured Liza. "You're in good hands! And you know, we're all here for you."

"Fuck!" Tina finally added to the conversation.

Liza jumped. "What?"

"Nothing, that shit just pisses me off!" Tina's voice shook. Everyone knew Tina's displays of concern and affection often came out in the form of curse-laced outbursts.

Liza smiled. "Cancer pisses you off? It should!"

The girls all rallied around their friend and unleashed a barrage of praise for Liza's indomitable spirit and positivity because she caught it early and was moving ahead swiftly with treatment. By the end of the evening Liza felt more confident that all would go well, and the girls were determined to spend more precious time together.

"Thank you all. I am so blessed to have you as my friends!"

"Yes, we're *Steel Magnolias*!" Julie shouted.

"Only steelier!" added Sarah.

"Ick!" Tina rolled her eyes.

The next time the girls met was at the hospital to support Liza through her surgery. *What a great fucking Christmas present*, thought Silvia. It was an early morning surgery so each of them was up and out the door by five o'clock. They were all sitting in the waiting room at around seven when Liza was brought in on a gurney ready to be rolled into surgery.

"You got this, Liza." Sarah tried to sound cheerful.

Silvia looked into the glassy eyes of her friend. "We're all praying for you. We'll be right here . . . love you."

"You're going to be fine." Julie patted her hand.

Tina blew Liza a kiss and then held prayer hands in front of her face.

"Thank you, my girls . . ." Liza was very relaxed after having been given a sedative. "I love you all and I'll see you later. Gotta do more comedy, right?"

The girls were grateful to see her before the surgery but were a bit unnerved by her vulnerable condition.

"Just a little off the top, Doc . . . ba dum bum!" Liza's joke and her imitation of drums cut the tension and made everyone laugh out loud. Then giggling herself, she waved and was wheeled away.

"We love you, Liza."

The girls sat down and settled in to wait for Liza to come through surgery. Some of her family were occupying a waiting room down the hall; however, the girls wanted to keep their own pain, prayers, and conversations among themselves. They talked and read and paced—anything to pass the time.

"Hey, Tina have you seen your nice old lady friend lately?" Sarah was playing with her phone.

"Mrs. Klein? Yes, I have. This week she came in with some homemade apple pie for me and told me I was too thin. How nice was that?"

Silvia smiled. "N-i-c-e! So how was the pie?"

"And why didn't you share?"

"It was dee-licious! Ha-ha! And for the record, there's no such thing as too thin in my business."

Sarah grinned. "You and Mrs. Klein—adorable! It's just so unlike you to show . . . warmth."

"Yes, very unlike me. I know what a monster I can be . . ." Tina stuck her tongue out. "So, how's Whiskey Sour? Do you have any pictures on your phone?"

"Of course!" Sarah smiled and began zipping through dozens of photos of her dog in various poses and different outfits. The three girls passed her phone around looking at the adorable pictures.

As the long hours waiting in that tiny room dragged on, everyone took turns stepping out into the fresh air and making trips for food to the vending machines and the cafeteria. At around two o'clock, Thomas came in and surprised the girls.

"I called but, of course, they wouldn't tell me anything, so I decided to stop in to check. Any news?"

"No, not yet."

"I wish I could stay but I have a meeting around the corner that I'm already late for . . . Would someone please call me when you hear anything?" Thomas stopped and motioned with his fist defiantly. "She just has to be okay." His eyes filled up with tears. "She just has to be—" He blew them all kisses, then waved and ran off down the hall.

By five o'clock the girls were exhausted and worried. Could something have gone wrong during Liza's surgery? Finally, Julie stood up and began to shake.

"What if . . ."

"What?" Silvia was jolted out of her slumber.

"What if she dies?" Julie had tears streaming down her face. "I mean, no one is saying it but . . . I think we're all afraid . . . What if she ends up dying from this?"

"She's having a panic attack." Sarah put her arms around Julie.

"Hey!" exclaimed Tina. "I don't think we should say things like that out loud, right Sil?"

"That's right."

Tina panicked. "Should we do that spitting thing Liza does?"

"Yes! Quick. Everybody spit!" ordered Silvia.

"Pooh, pooh, pooh!" The girls all spat three times into the air just as a nurse came into the room.

"Now the food here isn't that bad . . ." The nurse joked even though she was unaware of what just happened.

Silvia's face turned red. "Oh, we're so sorry. It's a bad luck thing. Never mind."

"No worries." The nurse smiled. "I just informed the family, and I can tell you as well, your friend is out of surgery and in recovery. The surgery went well." Cheers erupted from the friends, followed by more tears and deep sighs of relief.

"She'll probably sleep all night, so you should all go home and check in again tomorrow."

Drained and grateful that Liza was safe, the girls put on their coats to leave.

"We spit just in time," said Tina, "and don't anybody tell Liza I said that!"

On the way out, Silvia stopped in the hospital chapel and knelt at the tiny altar. "Thank you," she whispered, then blessed herself and dialed Thomas's phone number.

Chapter 16

NEW YEAR'S EVE CAME AND went without the usual celebration by the friends. Liza's surgery had taken its toll on everyone's emotions, so the girls decided to lay low this year. As she convalesced, Liza's two diminutive, look-a-like aunts insisted on nursing her back to health themselves and forbade any unnecessary stimulation. Did they think the girls would make her wrestle or play dodgeball if they visited? During this time, they all kept in touch by phone, and with every conversation Liza sounded stronger and more like herself. She had been working on some new jokes to pass the time but testing them out on the aunts proved meaningless because the crazy aunts laughed at anything. She often referred to them as "Arsenic and Old Lace."

When the aunts had finally gone home, the girls announced they would be coming over for a girls' Thursday night dinner and bringing Liza the meal of her choice.

"Anything you want," said Silvia. "Just tell me."

"Okay, let me think. Oh, I know. I want the broiled scallops with asparagus and squash from Leonardo's. Can I have that?"

"Absolutely. Sounds perfect."

As promised, on Thursday the girls showed up with food from Leonardo's and some wonderful pinot grigio.

"Here we are!" Julie entered smiling and carrying in some bundles. The other girls followed with the rest. "Hello!"

"Yay!" shouted Liza. "First come here and give me a kiss. I missed you all so much!"

They put down the take-out cartons and ran over to Liza, hugging and kissing their beloved friend. She smiled and reveled in all the love and attention. "Just be careful of my chest."

Tina stood back. "You look so good! You lost weight too, huh?"

"Yes, I did. As a matter of fact, I'm down almost twenty pounds."

"Wow, that's great!" Silvia looked her over too. "And your coloring! Everything looks great. I'm so happy this is over."

Julie kneeled next to her. "Is it over?"

"Yes. They said they were sure they got it all since it was only a speck, and they took all the breast tissue they could. And there was no sign of cancer in my lymph nodes."

"Yay!" They all cheered.

Liza clapped. "And in three to six months I'll be healed and ready for my implants."

"What's in there now?" Sarah tilted her head. "I see bumps."

"Expanders. They're like placeholders so the skin can heal while keeping space for the implants. And when the time is right, I get my new titties!"

"You gonna get giant bazongas?" Tina joked.

"No, I've had giant bazongas my whole life! I think I'm just going to go with what the doctor suggests given my body size at the time. Something not so . . . badda boom, ya know what I mean?" She giggled and held her hands out mimicking giant breasts.

"Oh Liza, I'm so happy for you." Silvia leaned in to hug her again.

"So no chemo or radiation?" asked Julie.

"No. They were certain they removed all of the breast issue they could so I don't have to do either one, and my oncologist agreed."

"Even better!" Julie raised her fists in the air.

Silvia got up. "Excellent! I'm so happy! I want more wine now!"

The wine was passed around and everyone filled their glasses.

"To Liza!"

"To me!"

"Fucking right!" said Tina. "Don't mess with the Queen of Comedy!"

Liza squealed and clapped at the generous reference.

"Thank God." Silvia whispered. She was suddenly overcome with how blessed they all were and had an intense need to honor this occasion.

"Girls, let's take a minute to acknowledge how blessed we are. Liza is better, and we're all together again and healthy! And that's the most important thing. Here's to this incredibly special moment together. Right now."

As the girls began eating their celebratory dinner, each one glanced around the sunroom. They seemed to look with fresh eyes at the pillows, the giant shoe, the macramé chair, and even the dancing girl painting, overcome with the soothing feeling of being home again after a long absence. They felt relaxed and safe again. They were all happy to get back to being an atypical, loving, wacky little family.

Liza lay on the couch. "I'm so happy we're all here! Shalom!"

"God bless us every one!" Julie murmured.

Tina rolled her eyes. "Why do you have to say shit like that?"

That Saturday, Liza decided she wanted to venture out a little and asked her friends if they wanted to meet for breakfast. They were all free that morning, so everyone showed up early at their favorite breakfast spot. Once their meals arrived and coffee was ingested, they came back to life and began talking.

"Tina, why aren't you stabbing Sarah with your fork this morning?" Liza asked as Sarah dove for cover.

"Mrs. Klein died." Tina sat quietly stirring her coffee. The girls gasped in shock and were all saddened by the news.

Silvia tried to take her hand, but she pulled it away. "I know you cared about her. I'm so sorry."

"Yeah, I did, but she was just a client, so I don't know why this is bothering me so much. I'm so upset." Tears finally began to flow. She sniffled and wiped her nose.

"Well, she was a nice lady for sure," Julie smiled warmly.

Sarah nodded. "And she was your friend, so it's understandable you would be upset."

Liza leaned over to her. "You spent a lot of time taking care of her at the spa. I think you kind of loved her in your own way. And you always felt badly that she was alone so much. That's sad."

Tina held her napkin to her eyes. "I know. The mailman found her."

"Oh!" Silvia gasped and shook her head as though trying to erase an image from her mind.

"That poor woman." Liza bowed her head. "So terrible to die alone. Of course you'd be upset. And I think that's exactly what you feared would happen."

"She didn't deserve that."

Julie leaned on her elbow. "Poor thing. She didn't have anyone after her husband died?"

"Her sister died and all her friends moved away."

Silvia turned to Tina. "You don't have to worry about ending up like that. You have a big family and plenty of friends, and I'm sure you'll meet someone someday."

Tina stopped crying. "I'm not worried about that, and don't say that!"

Sarah touched Tina on the shoulder, but Tina wriggled away. "Say what?"

"Tina, are you afraid of not finding anyone to spend your life with? You're still so young. It'll happen. Don't worry." Liza tried to calm Tina's escalating mood.

"I'm not worried! You know, I do have other things in my life," Tina protested, "and other people. I date."

Sarah nodded. "When? You work constantly."

"It makes sense." Julie shrugged. "We all think about stuff like that. It's natural."

Sarah smirked. "Okay. When was the last time you had a date?"

"I date." Tina blew her nose. "I just don't go spilling my guts to you guys every time something happens in my life!"

"Then why don't you ever share that with us?" Liza thought about her question for a moment and then tried to be more sympathetic. "Is it because he's maimed or deformed in some way? Or is he . . . special?"

"Liza!" yelled Silvia as the rest of the girls rolled their eyes.

Silvia tapped her fingers on the table. "Well, good then. So, when was the last time you went on a date?"

"You never talk about anyone. I don't remember you ever telling us a good or bad date story—the kind I always share!" Julie crossed her arms.

"Yeah, you share constantly! I don't like to—"

"Why the hell not?" Liza was insulted by the perceived slight. "That's not fair. We tell you everything."

Tina sighed, feeling pressured and frustrated. She reached for more coffee, and then sat up in the booth. "I was upset about Mrs. Klein, that's all. Why are you guys grilling me?"

The girls stayed quiet which made Tina even more uncomfortable.

"I don't like to . . . Look, when I first met you guys, I didn't feel as though I . . . fit in."

Liza hit the table with her hand. "How dare you! I have always made you feel included. Is it because you're Chinese? You know I love Chinese food and Chinese people!"

"What are you talking about, Liza?" Silvia sighed deeply.

"And I love those fucking fortune cookies too!"

"Okay. Enough with the fucking fortune cookies!" Tina paused for a moment. "Oh my God, I can't believe I'm doing this." She began to fidget in her seat and took a deep breath before speaking again. "When I first met you guys, all you ever talked about was going out with guys and sex and stuff."

"Well, we were young . . . er," said Julie.

"You all had this sense of humor where you made wisecracks about everyone who was . . . different. It was funny—don't get me wrong—but back then, it wasn't clear to me how you all really felt deep down . . . about certain kinds of people."

"I can't believe you were uncomfortable around us." Sarah shook her head. "Not you!"

"I'm confused—" Silvia scratched her head.

Tina sat up and put her hands on the table. "Let me finish, or I won't be able to say it." She took a deep breath. "It wasn't until Liza introduced Thomas to us that I ever really saw your . . . tolerance for certain people." She emphasized the word "tolerance."

"We're just always joking around." Liza threw her hands up. "That's all it is. We've always been very misunderstood."

"What are you talking about? We're tolerant—" Silvia stopped. She suddenly realized what Tina was trying to tell them. Looking straight at her, Silvia leaned in closer. "Are you trying to say that . . . you're gay?"

Everyone looked at Tina.

"Yes." Tina released a deep sigh and dropped her head. "And I've been in a relationship with someone for a while!"

"What?!" Liza banged on the table. "But you dress so—"

"Liza!" The girls screamed, and then began to process Tina's news.

Sarah tilted her head. "So, you thought if you told us we wouldn't accept you?"

"No, not really. Well, I wasn't sure in the very beginning," Tina explained. "I was always just used to not sharing that part of me. After a while, it just became harder and harder to say it. Of course, after I got to know all of you, I knew you were great women . . . but so much time had passed I just felt stupid blurting it out."

Julie leaned back. "So, you let us think, all this time, you were—"

"Asexual," said Liza. The girls shook their heads in disbelief. "I'm sorry, but I did wonder. I mean . . . there was nothing."

Silvia clasped her hands. "Oh! That is so sad . . . feeling like you had to hold that in. But now . . . It's so wonderful! You have someone you love! Tell us about her. Tell us everything!"

Everyone giggled and huddled together eager to hear every detail about Tina's relationship. Relieved now, she began to tell her friends about her girlfriend, Lynn. She even pulled out her phone and showed them a picture of the two of them together. By the end of breakfast, the girls were all happy to be closer to her, and she felt incredible.

Liza shook her head. "I just can't believe that all this time you never said anything. I still don't get why you didn't tell us when you met Thomas?"

"What was I supposed to say after a year or so of not telling you? 'Hey ladies, I have to come clean because Thomas saw me at one of the meetings, and I'm afraid he'll out me?'"

"Ha! Stupid!" Liza giggled.

Sarah shook her head. "You can sure keep a secret! We had no clue."

"I know. I had no idea because you dress so—"

"Liza!"

"It's no big deal, really. I'm used to hiding everything about my life from my family. But it does feel like a weight has been lifted, I have to admit." Tina stretched out her arms.

Liza clapped. "Good! Now, when can we finally meet this shiksa goddess?"

Julie jumped up. "How about at my wedding?"

The table went silent for a moment, and then an eruption of excitement startled the whole restaurant.

Julie shrieked. "Yes, we set a date. It's April twenty-fifth!"

Liza shook her head. "Another one that can hold on to a secret."

As the girls squealed at all the wonderful news, the patrons in the restaurant began to get annoyed with the noisy waves of emotion coming from their table.

Turning to face the ugly stares, Liza raised her coffee. "Folks, we're young, alive, and killin' it, so bite me!"

After breakfast, Tina had to go to work. Before it got too busy, she looked around the spa and could almost picture Mrs. Klein sitting quietly in a salon chair with her hands folded in her lap and a gentle smile on her lips.

The day went on without a hitch, and at around one o'clock she began wondering what to eat for lunch. Just as she stood up to leave her office, the phone rang and the receptionist told her two men were waiting in the foyer to see her.

Two men, Tina thought. *Can't be immigration, I was born in Poughkeepsie.*

She walked toward the foyer and saw the two men but didn't recognize them. "Can I help you gentleman?"

"Are you Tina Chin?" asked one of the men.

"Yes. How can I help you?"

"I am Charles Engels, and this is my associate, Edward Anderson. Is there someplace we can talk? Do you have a few minutes to spare?"

"Yes, sure." She turned and began walking toward her office. "Can I ask what this is about?"

"Nothing to worry about, ma'am. We here to tell you good news," said Mr. Anderson.

Ma'am, she thought. She took a few more steps and then suddenly stopped and turned to face the two men. "Wait. By good news do you mean spreading the good news like the Bible or religion? Because I don't have time—"

The men laughed and looked at one another. "I'm sorry. No, nothing like that."

As they filed into her office, Tina motioned for the men to sit down. Charles Engels got right to it. "I believe you were acquainted with Mrs. Klein. Is that correct? And you know she recently passed away."

"Yes." She became worried about how she died. "Are you detectives?"

Mr. Engels smiled. "No, Mrs. Klein was a client of ours. We're attorneys."

"Attorneys? Is there a legal issue concerning the spa?"

"No," said the attorney. "This matter doesn't concern the spa. We took care of Mrs. Klein's personal financial matters."

"Oh, really." She tipped her head sideways. "Sorry . . . I'm still confused."

"We're here to see you, Ms. Chin. See, Mrs. Klein was a very wealthy woman. She left the bulk of her estate to charity—well, lots of charities really. She also bequeathed a small amount to be divided among her staff and close friends."

"Estate? Staff?"

"Yes, Ms. Chin. Mrs. Klein considered you her friend." Mr. Engels smiled. "You see, Mrs. Klein was very fond of you. Wait, let me show you what she wrote. Go ahead, Ed."

Wrote? Tina's heart was racing. *Oh my God, what's happening?*

Edward Anderson rifled through some papers and found what he was looking for. "Mrs. Klein wrote," he read through the letter sporadically, 'That wonderful girl took a genuine interest in me. She's an extremely intuitive woman, never one to be fooled by posturing or false promises. She always has a smile and a laugh for me and goes out of her way to take care of me . . .'" He paused. "'No one has shown me such kindness in many years . . .'"

"Oh," Her eyes filled with tears. "She's so sweet."

Mr. Anderson then read from a separate document whose title was written in large letters: WILL. "I hereby bequeath—"

"Wait . . . bequeath, Mr. Anderson?" She stopped weeping and sat straight up.

"Yes, and please call me Ed. Mrs. Klein was a wonderful, generous woman and because of that . . ." Ed handed the document to Tina. "She left a little something for you. Read right here." He pointed to a highlighted paragraph.

Her head was spinning and her heart was pounding. After reading a few words, her mouth fell open. "What exactly does this mean?"

"It means you're receiving three million dollars from Ida Klein's estate!" Mr. Engels smiled. "Congratulations!"

Three, three . . ." she stammered, "three million dollars?"

"Yes," said Ed. "We know, given her total worth of fifty million, that's just a small endowment, but she wanted you to have something to help you—"

"Oh my God! Oh my God!" Tina screamed and began jumping up and down and hugging Mr. Engels and Ed for bringing her such wonderful, unexpected news. Once she calmed down, they finished up by getting her signature on some paperwork and, of course, discussing the details about the deposit. Then, they all shook hands and said their goodbyes.

Alone now, Tina fell back into her chair and put her feet up on the desk. She re-read her copy of the will and closed her eyes while tears streamed down her face. *Holy shit!*

Chapter 17

AFTER A FEW SHOWERS IN the morning, it was turning out to be a lovely day. The bride was grateful for the improvement in the weather and thrilled her big day had finally arrived. She paced back and forth in her bedroom, and with every other turn she took another glance in the mirror. *Wow*, she thought. *I'm really getting married today!*

Julie had taken her time choosing a wedding dress. She considered some of the dresses offered to her by family members, including her aunts and her mother, but none of them came close to fitting her tiny frame. She finally settled on a gorgeous ivory, tulle, and lace wedding dress with a sweetheart neckline and beaded sequins. On her head she wore a stunning diamond tiara that matched a simple diamond necklace given to her by her parents. Beautiful diamond earrings from her sister completed her wedding ensemble which made her feel like a storybook princess.

While she waited for the limousine to arrive, she tried to calm her nerves by taking deep breaths and remembering how much she loved her husband-to-be. She also listened to the voices of her relatives downstairs in the living room recounting all the great times Julie and her cousins had together and some of the boyfriends who had come around over the years. Because Julie was one of the youngest cousins to get married, the aunts and uncles began to fret over the fate of their own daughters.

"I keep telling my Suzanne to get herself into the city," said Aunt Jane. "She works and goes to the gym, then wastes her time going to bars with her friends here in the suburbs."

"The money's in the city!" shouted Uncle Frank. "If she wants to find a successful man, she's got to go to Manhattan!"

"Maybe do some charity work there—"

"Exactly!" confirmed Aunt Marion. "Why don't they get it?"

Suzanne screamed from the kitchen. "Mom, stop!"

"Listen to us for once!" begged her mother.

Uncle Frank began to pace. "So how's Brenda doing?"

"Brenda is right here!" Brenda peeked out of the kitchen.

"She's doing very well at her job but her social life . . . Well, I don't know," said Uncle Richard.

"Remember the one with the motorcycle?" asked Aunt Cathy. "My God, I thought my husband was gonna kill him. One night, he comes to get her on that monster. It was so loud, and it was late . . . almost nine o'clock and—"

"I ran out and told that kid no way my daughter's getting on thing!"

"That was years ago, Dad! I'm with Dougie now. What about Dougie?" Brenda yelled again from the kitchen. "I thought you liked Dougie!"

"Dougie's a nice boy," Aunt Cathy explained. "She dates Dougie now, but he's a landscaper, I mean—"

"He owns his own landscaping business, Ma! Will you just stop talking?!"

"So how are Mary Beth and Kelly?" asked Aunt Cathy.

"Mary Beth is actually dating a nice guy—a lawyer. He's a little OCD for my taste, but she really seems to like him," said Uncle Gene. "I get the feeling his long hours make Mary Beth think he's cheating. She's very suspicious by nature. I tried to explain that when these young guys are associates, they have to work long—"

"Dad!" screamed Mary Beth from another room.

Aunt Terry elbowed her husband. "Tell them about Kelly now."

"Oh, Kelly's going with this fellow—"

"Colin."

"Colin. He's working at the mayor's office in the city. I think he may have political aspirations, that one," said Uncle Gene. "The kid is sharp, I'll give him that."

"Yes, and he's just crazy for Kelly," bragged Aunt Terry.

"Yeah, I know what he's crazy for—"

"And Kelly would make an excellent senator's wife. Am I right?"

After more speculation about the fates of their children, the focus of all this talk came into the living room. The cousins had been gathered in the kitchen drinking wine and listening to their parents crucify their love lives.

Brenda stood in front of her parents with her hands on her hips. "Are you guys done now?"

"Yeah, please don't talk like this at the wedding. It's embarrassing!" said Suzanne.

Before things got heated, Julie's cousin, Michael, came running into the room. "The limo's here."

"The limo's here! The limo's here!" called the aunts as they got up and began to gather their belongings.

"We'll head outside." Uncle Frank motioned for the other men to follow.

Upstairs, Julie's sister and maid of honor, Jennifer, knocked on her door and then stuck her head in. "The limo's here."

"I heard." Julie peeked out the window at all the commotion. "Our poor cousins! Did you hear all that talk?"

Jennifer laughed and nodded. "Yeah!" She then paused, looking at her sister's outline in the window. "You look beautiful, Julie." Her sister's eyes filled up as the two hugged.

"Thank you. You do too. I told you that color would look amazing on you." She held her sister's arms out.

"You ready, girls?" Her mother's head popped inside the open doorway.

"Yes, Mom. Can you please get the uncles to get in their cars and go so I can get in the limo and leave in peace? I don't want everyone seeing me yet."

"Sure, dear."

Julie and Jennifer watched out the window as her mother hollered and directed all the aunts, uncles, and cousins to get into their cars and head to the church. The front yard looked like a crowded car dealership, leaving no way for any other vehicle to enter the property. Finally, with everyone in their cars and waving out the windows, they drove off like a parade without the giant floats.

As the last car made its way onto the street, a beautiful white stretch limo was able to pull in front of the house. Following her sister, Julie turned to leave her bedroom, but stopped to take one last look at herself in the mirror. *I can't believe this is me.*

Downstairs, her mother and father gathered their things then helped Julie down the front steps and into the limo. Julie and Jennifer sat on one side and their parents sat across from them. Once on the way to the church, her father popped a bottle of champagne and poured a little bit into four glasses.

"To my beautiful girls!" he toasted.

"To love," added her mother.

"To my family . . . I love you," said the bride. "Now, let's get me married!"

At the church, Julie, her mother, and sister stayed hidden inside what her sister called "the bride's dressing room." While her sister fixed her sophisticated chignon, her mother tended to her stunning violet Dolce and Gabbana silk gown which highlighted her blue eyes and lovely skin. Her father, who was too nervous to stay in one place, decided to go out on the steps of the church and keep an eye out for the groom because Zack wasn't there yet.

"I don't think Daddy believes Zack will show up." Julie giggled.

"I know!" her sister teased. "What if he doesn't?"

Her mother began fixing Julie's dress. "Oh, don't be silly. Your father's just anxious and needed something to do. Zack will be here any minute."

As the time for the ceremony grew near, her mother became weepy and nostalgic. "I remember the day you were born . . ." Her mother was beginning to reminisce about years gone by.

"I would hope so!" her sister laughed.

By the time her mother began telling stories about her teenage years, they could hear her father running down the hall. "He's here! He's here!" The three women laughed.

The door opened and her father entered smiling from ear to ear. "He's here, darling!"

"We heard, Daddy." Her sister kissed her father's cheek. "Wasn't the groom supposed to be waiting for the bride to arrive?"

"When has anything I've done ever been normal?" Julie chuckled.

"I know. I mean, you're marrying a man you met during a fight with a llama!" Everyone laughed.

"You know, Silvia told me right there in the ladies' room at the zoo that she bet he was the one." Julie smiled and nodded.

"Really? She said it that first day?" Her mother's eyes were wide.

"She knew he was special, and when we came out of the ladies' room and he was holding flowers for me, I think I knew too." She held her hand to her forehead and pretended to faint while her sister giggled.

"Well, he showed up. It looks like you're really getting married today!" her sister teased.

"You ready?" Her father was beaming at his beautiful daughter.

"Yes, Daddy. I'm ready."

The door opened again, and a church staffer announced it was time to begin. "Let's take our places, shall we?"

Her father put his arm out and Julie linked her arm with his. She noticed how distinguished he looked in his sophisticated black Tom Ford tuxedo. Her mother quickly checked her make-up in a mirror, then kissed her gently on the cheek and headed into the main church. Her sister took her place in front of the bride, and Julie and her father walked slowly into position, waiting for the signal to start down the aisle.

The organ began to play, and Julie and her father looked lovingly at one another.

"Daddy—" Julie began to cry.

"Stop. You'll ruin your make-up. I know, my dear daughter, I love you too."

The reception was jubilant. The girls felt like VIPs, dressed to the nines and having been assigned to the best table in the house—the one right in front of the dance floor. Liza was decked out in a show-stopping, mid-length, black sequined dress with matching shoes and bag. She was accompanied by the exquisitely dressed Thomas who, with his lively personality and great dance moves, made the perfect date.

Silvia and Sam came together. Silvia was wearing a lovely, blush-colored Theia teardrop mini dress, and Sam was sporting a gorgeous black Canali suit that Silvia had picked out.

Sarah entered the reception hall by twirling in front of her friends, showing off her flowing, black, off-the-shoulder gown. Her date, Jim, was a bank executive whom she met at work.

Finally, Tina and her girlfriend, Lynn, arrived in a black limousine and were both dressed in lovely coordinating Valentino cocktail dresses.

Lynn was being introduced to the group for the first time, so Tina was a bit nervous. After talking with her for five minutes, the girls understood why Tina loved her. Lynn was a lovely, sensitive woman with a lot of patience and a killer sense of humor. Everyone thought the two were a perfect match.

After the newlyweds were introduced to the guests as husband and wife and the formalities were satisfied, the celebration began. Everyone started socializing, moving from table to table until the waitstaff entered the hall and began distributing the meal. The menu was a feast of Caprese salads, shrimp cocktail, filet mignon, and salmon filet with roasted asparagus and scalloped potatoes, followed by strawberry cheesecake and a chocolate fountain. The champagne and wine flowed freely while the music, which was provided by a DJ friend of Zack, began playing some dinner music consisting of slow, melodious oldies. Once the waitstaff began clearing dinner plates, the DJ announced it was party time and switched to the latest, top of the charts dance music.

As soon as the girls heard the beginning notes of Lady Gaga's "Let's Dance," they hit the dance floor with their smoothest moves. They danced as a group and in circles around the bride and groom. They laughed and jumped around each other and during slow songs swayed with their dates. They even begrudgingly took part in the Macarena and did the chicken dance with some children. The DJ played everything from Diana Ross & the Supremes to Billie Eilish, and the girls sang every note and moved to every beat.

In between dancing and staggering up to the bar, the girls returned to their table to rehydrate with a little water and rub their sore feet. Hidden by the lovely white linen tablecloth, under the table a pile of high heeled shoes grew taller after every dance song. During each respite, the girls reminisced and told funny stories and even mocked some of the other guests.

Tina pointed across the room. "See that woman over there wearing the green slutty dress?"

"The one with the deep V in the front? Like the one J.Lo wore years ago to the awards?" Lynn rolled her eyes.

"Oh, that one," Sarah moaned. "Yeah, I thought it looked familiar. Wow, I would never have the guts to wear that, would you?"

"You could try." Jim leaned in closer to her and smiled.

"Never in a million years. On me, what was supposed to be in one spot would pop out in another spot." Silvia pointed to her various body parts.

Tina shook her head. "No it wouldn't. They use body glue."

"Body glue?" asked Sarah. "I don't think Silvia trusts glue anymore!" Silvia nodded and raised her glass while the girls chuckled again about Upside Down Jesus.

"Of course. How do you think her breasts stay in place . . . or that piece of fabric in the front stays put?"

"I thought it was just muscle tone." Sarah shrugged her shoulders.

Sam rolled his eyes as the girls talked about their lady parts.

"I'm going to the bar. Care to join me, Jim?" The two men smiled and retreated to a more male-oriented space.

"Oh, look over there," Silvia pointed at the newlyweds. "There's Julie and Zack dancing!"

"I know I just met them, but what a great couple they make," said Lynn.

"Just like us." Tina brushed her hand against Lynn's cheek.

Just then, Liza and Thomas came over and dropped into their seats. "Finally, a fucking slow song. Thank God!" Liza was breathing so heavily she could barely speak. "I can't get him to stop dancing."

Thomas wiped his sweaty face with a handkerchief. "I'm sorry if you can't keep up, Sista! I was made for dancing!" He then paused and sat up straight. "Oh my God, I have to request that song. Remember that one? Be right back."

"Wasn't that song by Leif Garrett?" Everyone stared oddly at Lynn for knowing that fact.

Silvia laughed. "She fits right in, Tina!"

"Oh God!" Liza kicked her shoes off and added them to the pile under the table. She began to rub her feet and moan. "Oh, that feels so good!"

"Tina told me that Julie and Zack met on the internet, and their first date was at the zoo, is that right? And Julie got sneezed on by a llama . . ." Lynn laughed at the crazy story.

Silvia nodded. "Yeah, I was there. It was disgusting, but I knew right away Zack was in love. I told Julie that day. I knew he was a good guy."

"Yeah, he's wonderful. I'll be back." Liza seemed distracted. She got up and hurried to the ladies' room in her stocking feet.

Silvia soon spotted someone interesting as well. "Oh, look at that woman over there. The lady with the really, really short haircut."

"The one who looks like a Tibetan monk?" asked Lynn.

Sarah looked over. "Wow, that's a really short haircut, am I right?"

"It is!" Tina made a stink face. "Not flattering at all. Who would ever get a haircut like that?"

"Lesbians." Silvia punched Tina lightly on the arm, and the friends all erupted in side-splitting laughter.

"You suck!" Tina giggled and shoved Silvia. "You know that, right?"

After a while, Thomas's song request was finally played. The girls jumped up and found him already dancing on the dance floor, so they formed a circle around him.

"I knew you would all come!" He danced while looking around for Liza and finally spotted her walking up to the DJ's table. As soon as the song ended, the girls could see her asking for the microphone, which sent them into a panic.

"She's not going to—" Silvia asked.

"Don't even say it."

"Hello, everyone," Liza began. "I just want to make a toast to Julie and Zack."

Tina bent forward and sighed. "That was fucking close!"

When he heard the announcement, Zack raced onto the dance floor and held his new bride in his arms.

"I am Liza Levy, the best friend of the bride."

"Well . . ." Silvia pretended to feel slighted by the comment.

Liza went on. "I'm just so happy these two magnificent people found each other. Our little group of friends—Julie's friends—feel so lucky to be here tonight and share in this blessed event. When Julie first told me she met a wonderful man named Zack and he might be 'The One,'" Liza explained using air quotes, "I got very worried my friend might have her heart broken because she seemed to have fallen in love so quickly. Then, one day, she asked me if I thought she would ever marry Zack. So, not knowing how to answer her, I made a joke—that's what I do—I said, 'Miracles you want? Better you should light a candle!' and Julie laughed. So, I said a prayer and did it for her . . . And here we all are!" Everyone applauded. "May Julie and Zack have a long, wonderful life together with much love and good fortune, and may the members of our girls' Thursday night supper club keep toasting one another until we're a hundred years old! Mazel, everyone. I love you, Julie and Zack!"

After everyone in the hall raised their glasses in tribute to the new couple, Tina leaned in to Silvia. "She sure loves the sound of her own voice."

"Yes, she does." Silvia smiled. "And it's one of my favorite sounds too."

Chapter 18

IT HAD BEEN ABOUT A month since Julie's wedding, and after a lot of rescheduling everyone was able to meet for dinner at Liza's. Tonight's menu was rack of lamb with lemon garlic butter, roasted potatoes, and green beans with pickled shallots and breadcrumbs and, of course, wine. By seven o'clock, the girls were enjoying themselves in the sunroom, except Silvia who they could hear walking slowly up the stairs. Liza, dressed in a long, silver sparkly top and black palazzo pants, jumped up to grab Little Bucket, but stopped.

"Hey. Silvia's not running up the stairs."

Sarah nodded. "Oh yeah. I hope everything's okay."

The door opened and in walked Silvia. "Hi everyone!" She closed the door behind her and took her place amongst the pillows. Everyone was staring at her.

"What the hell?" Tina threw up her hands.

"What?" Silvia stared back in confusion.

"You no upchuck?"

"Oh!" Silvia giggled. "Me no taxi. Sam drove me."

"That's just wrong!" Liza shook her head.

"What? You're mad because I don't feel like puking?"

"No, not mad . . . just disappointed." All the girls chuckled.

"So, Sam, huh?" Julie sidled up next to Silvia. "It sure took you two a while! Are you guys serious now?"

"Maybe," teased Silvia. "We don't really talk about it."

"Don't talk about what? Are you two a couple? What exactly are the carnival arrangements?" It was obvious Liza was interested in all the intimate details.

"You mean 'carnal'?" Silvia laughed. "We do what we do, that's all."

Julie smiled. "Are we asking too many questions?"

"Yes."

"Too bad. What happens if you find out he's sleeping with some-one else?" Liza was still curious.

"Well, he's not. We don't question each other and . . . Liza, would you like to hear about positions and frequency, or is that enough?"

She giggled and nodded. "Yes, I would!"

Though Silvia and Sam had been dating for a while, Silvia had been cautious about divulging any details until she was sure about Sam and, perhaps, in love. Things hadn't started to get serious until recently, and it felt good to keep a wonderful secret for a change. She knew that soon she would have to share her news with her best friends.

"Wow." Silvia changed the subject. "You really outdid yourself, Liza. This is incredible!" Everyone agreed as they began to devour the delectable meal.

Julie began telling everyone about her wedding experience and her glorious honeymoon in Greece while searching for a website on her phone. "If you go on this site, you can look at my wedding pictures. I'll send you all the link." Then she then began zipping through pictures of their trip on her phone.

"We saw the Acropolis. We went to the temple of Zeus, and to Lindos and St. Paul Beach. We went to Santorini and Mikonos . . . oh," she sighed. "It was just an incredible trip."

After enviable stories about the Greek islands, the conversation switched to the wedding reception.

"We had such a wonderful time." Liza popped some red hot candies into her mouth. "Thomas almost killed me though!"

Tina smiled. "That man can move, and he's so gorgeous!" The girls all looked at her.

"What? I can still appreciate a handsome man even though I'm gay, can't I?"

Liza rolled her eyes. "You know, you constantly fucking confuse me." The girls all laughed.

"I can't remember ever dancing so much in my life. We had a ball! And Sarah . . . oh my God, I've never seen you like that!" Liza swatted at Sarah.

"Like what?" She smiled coyly.

Silvia giggled. "You were like a drunken Cinderella before midnight! And you looked gorgeous!" Sarah smiled and shrugged her shoulders.

Julie poured more wine. "You met him at work, right? He's a banker?"

"Jim. Yes, he's a bank executive."

Silvia nodded. "Well, he seemed very nice. So, how's your job going? Do you miss old Combat Boots?"

"My job is great! And . . . I wasn't going to tell you guys this but, thanks to a brilliant idea from Tina, I left orally health-conscious Mary Louise with one hell of a good-bye."

The girls all looked at one another.

"Oh-oh. What does that mean?"

Tina dove into the pillow pile head first.

"Well, let's just say her big mouth got what it had coming to it, vis-à-vis, a funkified, toilet bowl dipped toothbrush!"

"E-e-e-w-w-w! You didn't!" Tina sat up and burst out laughing as Sarah shrieked with both pride and disgust.

"Tina!" The girls were horrified at first then slowly erupted into fits of laughter.

Finally, Liza spoke while still trying to catch her breath. "Girls, never make either one of them mad!"

"Anyway," continued Sarah, "we're taking it slow. We see each other every day at work and go out to dinner sometimes during the week. Then on Saturdays, I usually go to his house . . . and stay over," Sarah added unexpectedly.

"Slow my ass!" Tina pointed at Sarah. "Slut!"

"Finally! Another one I wondered about." Liza threw her hands up in the air.

Tina jumped up. "It's like you're a new woman! I can't believe it. And you're really smart! She calculates casualty rates and captivates corporate executives in a single bound, folks!"

"Cool!" Silvia chuckled as Tina stood up.

"Um, okay. I was waiting until after Julie shared her photos and we finished dinner to share some great news with everyone."

"Oh, how mysterious! What's up?" Julie smiled.

"I've been dying to tell you all this in person, but I didn't want—" Tina wiggled her body and had a huge smile on her face.

"My God. What is it?" Liza leaned forward.

"Alright. Ever since I first started working for Niki . . . Well, you all know I've always wanted to open a salon of my own some-day, and over the years Niki's been very supportive . . . teaching me everything she knew . . . for which I am extremely grateful—"

"Ya, ya, go on!" exclaimed Liza. "We know this part."

"Okay, so this past week, I thought Niki was acting a little weird. I figured it was because she knew I'd be leaving Santé soon because of the money I got."

"What's the news, dammit?" Liza was beside herself.

"The other day, Niki called me into her office. She told me her husband was still sick and she was going back to France to be with him very soon . . . for good. I think he may be dying."

"Oh, that's too bad." Silvia pressed her hands together. "So is she closing Santé?"

"Come on! Hurry up! I can't stand it!" Liza was freaking out.

"Fine! Niki asked me if I wanted to buy the spa!"

Liza gasped. "That's fucking amazing!"

"Get out!" Silvia jumped up and crashed into Sarah who was also trying to stand.

Julie smiled and clasped her hands. "Wow. That place is worth a ton of money. Can you? Buy it, I mean."

"Owning a place like that . . . Oh my God!" Tina looked up. "I've seen the books, and the business is worth a few million dollars. They could have asked for more, but Niki said she'd let me have it for just under one million."

"A million dollars?" Julie gasped.

"You're shitting me!" Sarah clutched her head. "I can't believe we're talking numbers like this."

"I spoke to those attorneys who gave me the gift from Mrs. Klein, and they agreed it was a solid business investment."

"So what did you say?"

"I said 'hell yes!'" Everyone jumped to their feet and hugged Tina.

"Oh, my God! We have our own salon! I think I'm gonna have a freakin' heart attack!" Liza fell back into her seat.

Silvia's eyes were teary. "Oh, Tina. This is amazing! It's your dream come true!"

Tina explained the basics of buying the spa to her friends, and after the shock wore off they began offering up ideas about her new business.

"Design it like a posh Indian palace."

"Have sale days!"

"Let your friends enjoy the services for free."

Tina laughed. "Thanks, Liza. You'd be there every day eating into my profits!"

"Yeah, but you'd have a relaxed and fabulous looking friend!" She giggled.

"Well, that's about it . . . gotta lot of work ahead of me." Tina relaxed on the pillow pile. "Oh, and . . . Well, Niki's only condition was that I change the name. So what do you guys think?"

"The Oasis."

"How about 'Body Beautiful'?"

"Why not just 'Tina's Day Spa'?"

Knowing Tina, Silvia knew she already had a name for her spa—probably picked out when she was eleven. "So, what is it?"

Tina closed her eyes and smiled. "Ciel. It means 'heaven' in French."

"Oh, I just got the chicken skin again!" Liza rubbed her arm. "That's perfect!"

Tina closed her eyes and smiled, basking in all her good fortune with her friends.

"Hey, think about it." Julie stretched out on the couch. "We have all really come a long way this year. Don't ya think?"

Liza nodded. "I know. Who could have seen all this coming?"

All of a sudden, Silvia stood up and began to pace back and forth. "You know what? You're right. Who could have—?"

Silvia then ran to a drawer in the kitchen and began scribbling on a piece of paper. After more wandering around, everyone became concerned.

"Sil, you alright?" Liza followed her around with her eyes.

Sarah got up to grab a cold water. "What are you doing?"

"Silvia, you're scaring us?"

"Oh my God!" Silvia stopped and kneeled down to face the girls.

Tina sat up. "What the fuck? I was all relaxed!"

"Do you guys remember the time we went to see Liza's friend in Massachusetts?"

Julie nodded. "Yes, when we went to see the witches!"

Two years earlier, the girls were having one of their Thursday night dinners when Liza told them she had received an invitation from a former co-worker. They were invited to go to Salem, Massachusetts, to attend an extravagant Halloween party. Having no plans that weekend and loving the idea of going to Salem at Halloween, everyone agreed it would be fun. They rented a car and hit the road that next morning.

They arrived at the Boston Marriott around dinnertime on Friday, and after checking into two rooms they headed across the street to an open tourist area called Faneuil Hall to find a place for dinner. The next day, they did some sightseeing around Boston. They walked the Freedom Trail, which highlighted the presumed route of the famous patriot Paul Revere in 1776, and through the Boston Commons. They even did some high-end shopping on Newbury Street.

By six o'clock they returned to the hotel to get ready for the party. At eight o'clock they headed out to Salem which was only about a half hour outside the city. They wanted to get there early to see the holiday sights before going to Liza's friend's house at the specified ten o'clock arrival time.

It was the day before Halloween and Salem was buzzing. There were crowds of tourists and townies alike dressed in costumes, taking trolley tours, and popping in and out of stores and pubs whose themes were all witch related. They walked by the House of the Seven Gables made famous by author Nathaniel Hawthorne's novel of the same name. They peeked into the shop owned by Laurie Cabot, a reported American witchcraft high priestess, and walked through the Salem Commons located in the historic district.

Just after ten, the girls arrived at the beautiful old house owned by Liza's friend, Priscilla. The house and surrounding yards were adorned with tiny lights and many glowing Halloween decorations. They entered the house and noticed that quite a few people were already there. As they stood in the foyer, Priscilla came rushing over to greet them.

"Oh my God, you made it!" Priscilla and Liza hugged for a while before moving into the main living area.

"These are my friends, Priscilla. This is Silvia, Julie, Sarah, and Tina." The girls greeted Liza's friend as they looked around her house buzzing with activity.

"Your house is magnificent!" Silvia shook her hand. "And the decorations—"

"Yeah, it's gorgeous!" Julie spun around pointing at everything.

"I'm glad you like it, and I'm so happy you were all able to come." Priscilla looked around and began explaining everything her guests might enjoy.

"Now, the buffet is over there. Help yourselves to the food— there's a ton to eat. Next to that is the bar where you can find just about anything." Then she turned and pointed to the back of the house.

"Back there are some of my friends. There is Simone, who is a tarot card reader— wonderfully spiritual woman. There is also Melinda, the palm reader, back there. She's also a healer. In that corner, you'll find Mary. She's a direct descendent of the 1690 witches who were burned because of their religious beliefs. She'll be telling stories about her family and other events that took place long ago. And . . . somewhere around here is my friend and next-door neighbor, Felicity. She's great . . . amazing woman. She's clairvoyant and reads energy, and I can't wait for you all to meet her." Priscilla turned back around.

"So, you girls can walk around, participate, sit and eat. Please do whatever you want. Enjoy yourselves. Liza, I've got to take you over to see Freddie. Come on! See you girls later!"

As Liza was dragged off by Priscilla, the girls huddled into a circle and discussed what they wanted to do.

Julie looked around. "I think I'm going over there to the tarot card reader. Maybe she can tell me when I'll meet Mr. Right."

Sarah made her eyes wide and spoke in a scary voice. "I'm going over to listen to the stories of Mary, the descendent of the witches."

Tina turned to Silvia. "What about you?"

"I think I'm just going to sit and have something to eat. That couch over there looks very comfortable. That's where I'll be if anyone needs me."

Tina nodded. "Not interested in anything?"

"Not really. I had one experience with this stuff when I was a kid. There was a man wandering around our neighborhood telling people how they were going to die and revealing their darkest, most personal secrets. Scared everyone. I mean, how could this stranger know that stuff? Anyway, my aunt called and said, 'If he ever comes near you, just close your eyes and picture yourself surrounded by white light. That will block him from your mind.'" Silvia felt uncomfortable as she looked at the stunned faces of her friends.

Tina laughed. "Seriously?"

"Yeah. So, I practiced doing that in case I ever saw him, but I never did. My aunt claimed it was an old Mediterranean belief that some people have special powers—kind of like a witch doctor. They have the ability to read your mind and use your weaknesses against you."

"Wow." Julie was dumbstruck.

"Anyway, he disappeared a few days later. So this stuff kind of freaks me out."

Sarah raised her eyebrows. "So you believe in it?"

"Not in it, but after hearing tons of stories from my father's side of the family, I just don't want to encourage or insult it either. I don't want to hear anything about me or my future. I'd rather be surprised—the way God intended!"

Tina thought for a moment, considering her options. "Well, I'm going over to the palm reader. That looks harmless enough. I think I'll watch for a while . . . maybe get a reading. Girls, let's all meet Silvia later at the couch over there."

Everyone agreed and scattered around the house. Silvia went over to the buffet and reviewed the selection of foods. It all looked delicious. She chose some steak tips and a handful of french fries, along with one half corn on the cob which she covered in butter and salt. She set her plate down on the table in front of the empty sofa and went over to the bar to grab a cold beer. Upon her return she made herself comfortable and slowly savored every bite of her meal while watching all the interesting things going on around her.

A few people stopped by to introduce themselves and inquire about her interest in learning about readings and exploring past lives. She politely thanked them for the offers but declined using a headache as an excuse for her lack of participation. After a while, a woman came over and sat next to her on the couch. She was enjoying an unprecedented second helping of french fries with her beer and said hello to the smiling woman.

"Those look delicious," said the woman. "I wish I could eat like that and look like you."

Silvia smiled. "Oh, thanks, but I never eat french fries. I'm cheating big time tonight!"

"Now, who are you friends with here, if you don't mind me asking?"

"My name is Silvia. I'm here with my friends from New York. My friend, Liza, used to work with Priscilla in New York City."

"Oh! Prissy told me you were coming. My name is Felicity. I live right next door. Nice to meet you." She held her hand out to Silvia.

"Nice to meet you too." As Silvia shook Felicity's hand, every hair on her body stood up.

"So you and your friends drove up from New York. Are you staying in Salem or in Boston?"

Silvia smiled politely. "We're staying in Boston. We did some sightseeing today and will probably head back to New York tomorrow afternoon." Felicity seemed to be watching her closely as she spoke.

"Sounds fun. Quality time with a best friend is so important. Sounds like you and Liza are as close as me and Priscilla . . . Two minds, one spirit, you might say."

"Um . . ." Silvia began to feel uneasy. "Yeah, we're having a great time."

"But I see you're not seeking any counsel from our sisters." Felicity was beginning to pry. Silvia struggled to think of a reason to excuse herself but didn't know where to go.

"That's perfectly fine, especially for a woman who is . . . strong and fearless." She smiled at Silvia as her hands hovered closely around her shoulders and back.

"Oh, thank you." Silvia wriggled in her seat while trying to finish eating.

"You are formidable, but you might benefit from knowing what might come your way."

"No, to be honest, I'd—"

Felicity laughed. "Prefer to let it all . . . unfold naturally?"

How the fuck? Silvia's heart began to race, and she felt a bit ill. She then saw Felicity's hands moving around her and threw politeness out the window.

"What are you doing?"

"Oh dear, I've made you uncomfortable. I'm so sorry. I didn't mean anything by it. Sometimes there's such an abundance of energy, I just can't help myself."

"Well, I'd appreciate it if you wouldn't do that."

After a few minutes, Felicity stirred again. "You have very positive energy, and you're very in touch with your spiritual side." Felicity stood up and put her hands lightly on the top of her head. "You're a successful . . . Wait, you have doubts—"

As Felicity stood motionless over Silvia, Silvia became desperate for this woman to leave her alone—and then she remembered the "white light" trick. She picked up her beer, relaxed her back against the couch, and closed her eyes. She imagined a giant sun shining on her, covering her entire body with light.

Felicity watched her and giggled softly to herself.

"Now will you stop?" Silvia stared straight at her and leaned away, defeating her bold move.

"As you wish." Felicity turned and slowly walked away. "Goddess has blessed you, Silvia. You are gifted. Don't waste it."

Silvia was physically shaking, and after she was sure Felicity had left the room, she went over to the bar and threw back a shot of tequila. She returned to the couch and settled down, hoping the girls would come back soon. After about an hour, Julie came back smiling from ear to ear.

"Well, I guess you got some good news." Silvia was thrilled to see her friend.

"Yeah, but it was kind of stupid. She told me some boring stuff and then she told me she saw me and my future husband on a farm!" Julie laughed. "Can you imagine me on a farm? So I guess I gotta move to Oklahoma! Well, it was fun anyway!"

As Julie shared a few other details, Sarah came over and sat down. "Well, that was really interesting. That woman, whether really a descendent or not, knows her stuff. What those poor women went through back then . . . Horrifying."

Silvia smiled. "So you had fun too?"

"I did, but strange, though. As I was leaving, she told me to watch out because I could trip over big shoes." She looked at her shoes. "I don't have big feet, do I? Is a size nine big? Now I'm self-conscious."

Tina, Liza, and Priscilla turned up next.

"Okay, well, I just wanted to say good-bye girls. I hope you had a good time. Thank you all for coming." Priscilla was being pulled away by some other friends. "Liza, we have to keep in touch, okay?"

"Okay!" She smiled and waved good-bye.

"So what happened to you two?" Silvia turned her attention to Liza and Tina.

"Well, I was told that a William or Bill . . . I don't know. Some guy would make my dreams come true. So I guess that's exciting." Tina rolled her eyes.

"And, Liza, did your friend take you to meet her husband?"

She laughed. "Husband! Freddie was her cat!" Everyone shrieked with laughter.

"What?!" Silvia covered her loud mouth.

"Yeah, she told me Freddie the cat was really her brother reincarnated! Can you believe that? And she told me Freddie wanted to come home with me and sit in my shoe! Oh, then I met her friend, Felicity. Did any of you meet her?"

The girls shook their heads as Silvia rolled her eyes.

"She was a hoot! She put her hands all around me and told me I was strong. So dramatic and spooky! Oh, and then she said something like after a fight people will be laughing . . . something like that anyway. At 220 pounds, I'm sure there'll be laughter if someone picks a fight with me! I swear everyone in this fucking place is meshuga!"

"At least the cat is—your fucking feet stink!" Tina made all the girls laugh.

"Oh my God!" Silvia shook her head clumsily.

Liza stared at her. "What happened to you? Are you drunk?"

"Oh yeah. A little. But I don't want to talk about it. Just please get me the hell out of here!"

After the girls recalled all the details of that crazy night, Liza looked at Silvia. "What made you think of that?"

"Don't you see? Oh my God!" Silvia stared at her notations.

"What?" Everyone huddled around her.

She paused and took a deep breath. "You guys, can't you see?"

Sarah shook her head. "You're not saying—"

"Hold on a minute. First, Tina. You were told a 'William' would make your dreams come true?"

Tina looked at her. "So? I haven't met a guy named William, or any guy. I'm gay remember?"

"I know! There was no guy . . . but there was a Will." Silvia whispered. "Mrs. Klein's will!"

Slowly, Tina's eyes grew wide and her mouth fell open. "Holy fuck!" She fell over into the fetal position.

"And you, Julie. The farm prediction?"

"Yeah, what about it. I'm married now and live right here in an apartment in good ole New York!"

Silvia smiled. "But the animals . . . didn't you first meet Zack at the zoo?"

Julie nodded her head and then grabbed the cushions on her seat. "Oh my God, my husband . . . the llamas!"

Silvia next looked at Sarah who shrugged her shoulders. "Okay. This is ridiculous. I sat and listened to old legends. I didn't get a reading."

"Think about it, Sarah. The woman did tell you to be careful not trip over big shoes." Silvia raised her eyebrows. "Who wears big, ugly shoes and was always tripping you up?"

Sarah thought for a moment then covered her mouth. "Fucking Combat Boots! No!"

"And Liza—"

"Stop it. This is weird! I didn't have a reading either. I just visited with my friend."

"Yes," Silvia smiled. "But what did your friend tell you?"

"Nothing. All she said was that Freddie the cat was her reincarnated brother and wanted to sit in my shoe!" She laughed.

"And her friend told you about laughing coming after a fight. Liza, you fought cancer and beat it ... And now you're doing stand-up ... and writing better comedy than before you had surgery."

Liza sat silent.

Silvia continued, "And has Priscilla ever been to your apartment?"

"No, never."

"Liza, turn around. Could that be where Freddie wanted to sit?"

Everyone turned slowly and stared at Liza's giant shoe chair in the window. After a moment, they all jumped to their feet and began screaming.

"I can't handle this!" said Liza. "I gotta go lie down!"

"I'm outta here!" Tina grabbed her handbag and headed for the door.

"Bye!" Sarah and Julie turned and ran down the stairs practically tripping over one another.

"Goodnight everyone!" Liza fell onto the couch and covered herself in a blanket.

Silvia smiled, sat back down on the floor, and looked at Liza's prone body all covered up.

"Can I do anything for you before I go?" Silvia chuckled.

"Yes! Call Father Donohue!"

Chapter 19

A FEW WEEKS LATER, SILVIA and Liza decided to meet on a Friday for lunch. Liza had to drop by Dr. Melvin's office for a check-up in the afternoon and suggested Silvia meet her downtown—a perfect way to end the week.

Silvia's morning wasn't that busy, and for some reason she just couldn't concentrate. At around eleven o'clock she called it quits and decided to surprise her friend earlier than planned. Liza's doctor's appointment was for one o'clock, so she had plenty of time to meet her there rather than at the restaurant.

On her way, Silvia passed some interesting stores and shops near the hospital. One exquisitely decorated window beckoned her to come in and look around. It was called Allure and featured ladies' clothing and accessories.

With time to kill, Silvia looked around at all of the beautiful outfits. She saw gorgeous shoes and unique handbags. She also flipped through the designer scarves where she found a lovely multi-colored scarf that reminded her of a French impressionist painting. She had to buy it.

She went to the register to pay for the scarf, and while looking through her wallet she looked down through the glass counter at the jewelry. There her eyes landed on the perfect gift for Liza. It was a small gold microphone adorned with tiny diamonds on a lovely long, gold marine chain. She called to the salesperson to take it out of the case. After examining the stunning eighteen carat gold piece, she pulled out her credit card, slid it to the salesperson, and asked for it to be gift-wrapped. Though she wouldn't ask the girls to pitch in, she felt she needed to ask them if they wanted to be included in giving it to Liza. After a few cell phone calls, they all excitedly agreed and insisted on dividing up the cost.

With the gift hidden deep inside her bag, Silvia continued on her way to the hospital to meet Liza. She was so excited about the charm that she had to fight the urge to give it to her immediately. When she arrived, she headed up to the fifth floor.

As she walked off the elevators on five, she checked the large information board for Dr. Melvin's suite number. She proceeded down the hall but was sidetracked by the sounds of laughter coming from a nearby room. Curious, she crept quietly to the room and peeked in through the small window in the door. There she saw a large group of patients and nurses who were focusing their attention on someone at the front of the room—it was Liza.

She entered the room undetected and took a seat in the back behind the lively, fixated audience. Through the crowd she saw Liza standing at the far end of the room wearing a large pink t-shirt and funny-looking sunglasses. Everyone appeared to be having a great time watching her tell stories and jokes. *Could she be performing for these people?* Silvia listened some more and soon realized that, although she had missed the beginning of Liza's monologue, she had luckily managed to catch some of the end.

"*I, myself, was just recently released from this hospital as some of you know. In case you can't see it, I'll read you what my shirt says. It says, 'Of course they're fake, my real ones tried to kill me!' [Laughter.] I think most of us here can relate. [Laughter.]*

"*So yes, I am a former breast cancer patient. Happy to be here . . . actually happy to be anywhere really! [Laughter.]*

"*When I first told my friend Thomas about my breast cancer, I didn't know what to say so I began by saying, 'Honey, there are a couple of things I need to get off my chest.' [Laughter.]*

"*And it was weird when I started telling people I had cancer because some of them began telling me their deepest, darkest secrets . . . like it was safe to unburden themselves to a person who most likely was going to die—no witnesses, right? [Laughter.] But I fooled them. I lived. And I think a couple of them shit themselves when they saw me alive on the street a couple months later! [Laughter.]*

"*I've been told that I was really high after being given those, you know, those relaxation drugs that they give you before surgery. Evidently I was more aware of what was happening than they thought because they told me I said to the doctor, 'Please stop the war in my rack.' [Laughter.]*

"*And unfortunately—or fortunately depending on how you look at it—I am a woman who is unmarried [Laughter] Not sure why that is funny—and had to go through this by myself. I mean, there are easier things in life than trying to find a good, supportive man . . . like nailing jelly to a tree, for example. [Laughter.]*

"*But there are men out there who are sensitive, caring, and good-looking. It's just that they already have boyfriends. [Laughter.]*

"Like my mother used to tell me about men—if he's a disgrace, you gotta replace! [Applause.] Kinda like breasts, I guess! [Laughter.]

"I don't mean to pick on men, really. There are the rare few ones that do finally manage to say those three magic little words—the words every woman wants to hear: You were right. [Laughter.]

"So I relied on my girlfriends for love and support [Applause.] And let me tell you, my friends might be a little crazy, but they're the greatest. I tell them, we are best friends. Always remember, if you fall, I will pick you up . . . right after I finish laughing! True, right? [Laughter.]

"Recently we embarrassed ourselves in a church during a memorial mass where person after person got up and said wonderful things about my dead uncle. Yeah, we got so silly—we couldn't stop laughing, and I literally peed in my pants! [Laughter.] Just a warning—these things can happen when crazy old women get bored.

"You know, people say laughter is the best medicine, but for me and my friends, we know that wine is a better way to go. [Laughter.] And I do try to stick to wine because vodka mixes too well with everything . . . except my decisions. [Cheers.]

"So as I leave you, I want to make sure you have really heard my message. The reason I stopped by was to share with you my own personal mantra: Stay strong, keep looking forward, and know that the breast is yet to come! [Laughter and applause.]

"And one more thing before I go. Remember, the right attitude means everything. A wise woman once said, 'Fuck this shit' and she lived happily ever after. Thank you!"

When Liza took her bow, the crowd applauded wildly.

"Oh, thank you, dear women!" She clapped along with her makeshift audience. "My prayers are with you. Thank you for having me. I love you all!"

As she made her way toward the exit at the back, she was shocked to see Silvia standing there. "Oh! How . . . What are you doing here?"

"Took a half day . . . Thought I would surprise you." Silvia smiled. "But it looks like you surprised us both."

Chapter 20

WORD SPREAD LIKE WILDFIRE ABOUT Liza's performance for the breast care patients at the hospital. Soon, many people from all over began reaching out to her, encouraging her to continue her foray into comedy. A couple of weeks later, she hosted another girls' Thursday night dinner. They were all anxious to see her and praise her recent success. This evening, she served an Italian feast of bruschetta, antipasto, baked stuffed shells with meatballs, and tiramisu for dessert. She was dressed in a vintage black Twofer midi dress with a long pleated bottom reminiscent of Italy in the 1950s.

As they gobbled up her delicious meal, Sarah, Julie, and Tina listened as Silvia described Liza's performance and hailed her effortless command over the "audience" at the hospital.

"I must tell you, when I saw Liza up there, I was shocked. She looked so relaxed and friendly—you know, just like she is with us. I couldn't believe it. She had the crowd in the palm of her hand, and everyone in the room was hysterical. I wish I had seen it from the beginning!" The girls were thrilled to hear how far she had come in bringing her dream to fruition. Liza was delighted and touched by their enthusiasm, love, and support.

Once the conversation slowed down, Silvia grabbed her bag and took out a small present. Liza's eyes lit up.

"Is that for me?"

"Yes, it is!" The girls all smiled and clapped.

"I was just kidding, but . . . it really is?"

"Yes, it's from all of us. Here, open it." Silvia handed Liza the beautifully wrapped gift.

She blushed and reached for the box.

"Open it, open it!" The girls were chanting, anxious for her to see their gift.

She slid the bow off and slowly removed the wrapping. When she got to the box, she looked at her friends nervously.

Silvia was dying from anticipation. "Open it for heaven's sake!"

She lifted the lid and gasped when she saw the stunning gold microphone charm and chain. She stared at her precious gift and tried to speak as tears rolled down her cheeks.

"Oh, I can't believe you girls did this! How did you even find this?"

"Sil found it. Oh my God!" Tina laughed. "I knew she would slobber all over it."

Julie looked into the box with Liza. "So do you like it?"

"It's so beautiful. I love it! Thank you all so much."

Silvia bent over and fastened the necklace around Liza's neck, then stood back and admired the beautiful piece of jewelry just meant to be worn by her beloved friend. It was the perfect complement to her outfit.

"So glad you like it." Silvia kissed her on the cheek.

"It's perfect!" Liza looked down and touched her charm and then remembered another special gift she received.

"Wait, girls. I have something too!" Liza ran over to her shelf and retrieved a long, tall gift box and brought it to the center of the group.

"Everyone, grab a hold." They all looked at one another, then reached in and ripped away the packaging unveiling the gift Thomas promised to send to Liza. It was a bottle of Tuscan Masseto red wine.

"Girls, Thomas sent this to me. It's delicious, and it costs three hundred dollars!"

Julie's eyes grew wide. "Oh my God! You sure you want to open that?"

"Fucking right! Let's open it!" Tina ran and grabbed a wine opener while Julie took some clean wine glasses out of the cabinet. Once the wine was poured, the girls reveled in its luxurious quality and taste.

"To us!" Liza smiled at her special friends.

The girls all raised their glasses to one another. "To us!"

After a few minutes of enjoying such a special treat, Silvia decided it was time for her news. "Well ladies, this is kind of perfect because I have an announcement." She grabbed her bag once again and pulled out a stack of papers. Everyone got quiet and turned to listen to Silvia.

"Why do we all love to make announcements at these things?" Tina smiled.

Liza giggled. "I know, right? What is it, Sil?"

"I got published! My first article is in *New York Family Magazine*!"

"Yes!" Sarah raised her fist. "That's great! Congratulations!"

"You did it! You did it! I'm so proud of you!" Liza jumped off the giant shoe and hugged her. "I told you. Oh my God!"

"Thank you, everyone. Thank you. I just happen to have a copy here for each of you." Silvia's face was flushed with pride and a little embarrassment as she distributed to her friends the actual magazine issue in print. "Okay, but don't open it yet!"

The girls stared at the magazine cover. Silvia wanted to explain how her article came about so her friends would understand what they were about to read. She lowered her eyes, took a deep breath, and spoke from her heart in a shaky voice.

"When I contacted the magazine, I wasn't sure if they would go for my idea. I started thinking that, besides the five of us, there must be other groups of close women friends who rely on one another for help and encouragement . . . for everything, really. The kind of relationships we have are vital to each of us—to our happiness, our successes, and our growth as good people. I thought, not every woman has a husband or family to help them carry the load. Sometimes women consider their friends as their family . . . like I do, and those friends are the most important people in their lives. I mean, I don't think I could survive without you guys."

Liza nodded. "So true."

"While I begin the article by describing all of that, I think the parts you'll be most interested in are a few paragraphs down from the top." She rubbed her hands nervously. "So go ahead and take a look at page seventeen."

As each of the girls got to the specified page, they reacted to the title first: "The Friends You Keep" by Silvia Cruz.

"Wow!" Liza looked up at Silvia. "Is this about . . . us? I'm going to cry."

Silvia giggled. "Just read it! Each of you read your part out loud!"

"I'm so nervous." Julie was shaking.

"This is fucking awesome!" Tina smiled at the title page.

Silvia smiled at their first impressions. "Okay, Julie, you go first!"

Julie began reading out loud. "'My friend Julie is a bright, delicate person who doesn't even realize her incomparable contribution to my life. She has the ability to awake each day with a blind eye to the past and a renewed faith in humanity. For years, she found the dating world to be an arduous place, though she approached every experience with painstaking preparation and infinite optimism. Her sweet nature and unassailable need to see the best in people always seemed to attract abusers, users, and self-obsessed men. Romance for Julie always ended in a broken heart and periods of self-exploration and self-loathing. It took a moment at her lowest point—literally, mortified and mucus-covered—for her genuine heart and sensitive spirit to be seen through the eyes of the right man and finally appreciated. I believe her to be Cinderella personified. No one deserves love and happiness more than my friend . . .'" Julie covered her face with her hands.

Sarah spoke next. "'My friend Sarah is a wondrously layered woman with an unassuming depth of character. She's strong and tough on the outside, perfectly suited for a profession supervising others and effortlessly accomplishing the impossible. However, deep inside her a restless alter ego smiles and waits patiently to meet its host. Come sundown and hair down, this loving, ever-pleasing soul relinquishes control over everyone and everything and becomes a part of the tides of life. Her true strength lies in her appreciation for and ability to transform into a relaxed, joyful, enthusiastic participant in the mayhem and madness perpetuated by the people fortunate enough to be called her friends . . .'" Sarah blinked her eyes trying to hold back tears.

Silvia then pointed to Tina. "'My friend Tina is a dynamo. Her maquillage and tiny frame house unexpected gifts. Her immense creativity and boundless imagination are astounding, and her inherent kindness and compassion are bestowed on anyone in need of love. As a child, she dreamed of becoming an independent, self-sufficient woman, and her razor-sharp intensity and fearless drive enabled her to achieve that goal. Those close to her marvel at her determination and agility, overcoming obstacles without hesitation. In the presence of her radiating spirit, we are imbued with her passion which enables us to share in the depths of her verve and see clear the path necessary to make our own dreams come true . . .'" Tina turned away, speechless.

Silvia then nodded at Liza. "'My friend, Liza,'" she read tearfully, "'is a true blessing to her gender and an awe-inspiring force of nature. She is essential to my existence. She wanders through the world as an unexpected hero waking us all from passivity. She's a confluence of all that is good. She appears otherworldly, emitting an effervescent presence and the supreme charisma of people like Elvis and Marilyn Monroe. She's blessed with the coveted ability to charm and laugh the bad away. She's a joyful soul who appears before you, showering you with her special magic dust and blowing up the ordinariness of your life, leaving you spinning in her wind of love and happiness . . .'" Liza burst into tears.

After reading the beautiful tributes, the girls sobbed and hugged each other. They were all truly touched by Silvia's words and became more aware and appreciative of the wonderful relationships they shared. They sat together in quiet enjoyment feeling connected and blessed. Soon they realized it was getting late and were feeling weak and tired by the enormous displays of emotion.

"I'm calling it." Tina yawned and stretched. "I've got to go to work tomorrow. I can't believe we talked this much. It's after midnight. Thank you, Silvia. So proud of you."

Sarah stretched her body. "Me too. What a great night. Thank you again, Sil."

"Love you, Sil! Congratulations!" Julie kissed Silvia on the cheek.

"I am so glad you all appreciated the article. I wanted to tell the world how lucky I am—we are. I'm just thrilled the magazine agreed with my concept."

"It was truly a magical night," Liza clasped her hands at her chest. "Girls, I love you all. Let's have another night together soon. How about a month from now? I'll text you so we can all put it in our calendars before they fill up."

Silvia jumped up first and headed for the door. She opened the door and pretended to leave but had one more surprise to unveil.

"Have a nice night!" she called, then closed the door but lingered in the hallway. She listened to the voices of her dearest friends and giggled to herself anticipating their screams at what she was about to say. She took a deep breath and steadied herself. There was no turning back. After saying this, nothing would ever be the same again.

She took off her coat, put down her bag, and braced herself for the onslaught of questions, and thousands of hugs and kisses. "Oh girls!" she called as she opened the door again just enough for them to hear her. "I forgot to tell you one last thing. There's going to be a new addition to our Thursday night supper club. I'm pregnant!"

Printed in the USA
CPSIA information can be obtained
at www.ICGtesting.com
LVHW010718130424
777323LV00010B/435